Bean Me Up

Hunter,
your heart for people, ping-pong, and certs is Awesome!
God Bless your journey!

Lauren
Busbee
Jeremiah 29:11

Bean
Me Up

Lauren Busbee

TATE PUBLISHING
AND ENTERPRISES, LLC

Published by Tate Publishing & Enterprises, LLC
127 E. Trade Center Terrace | Mustang, Oklahoma 73064 USA
1.888.361.9473 | www.tatepublishing.com

Tate Publishing is committed to excellence in the publishing industry. The company reflects the philosophy established by the founders, based on Psalm 68:11,
"The Lord gave the word and great was the company of those who published it."

Book design copyright © 2015 by Tate Publishing, LLC. All rights reserved.
Cover design by Junriel Boquecosa
Interior design by Angelo Moralde

Published in the United States of America

ISBN: 978-1-68118-574-3
1. Fiction / Christian / Romance
2. Fiction / Action & Adventure
15.02.23

Those who hope in the LORD
will renew their strength.
They will soar on wings like eagles;
they will run and not grow weary,
they will walk and not be faint.

—Isaiah 40:31

To Kent,
my hero,
the one who always
holds my hand.

Acknowledgments

My thankfulness begins with God for inspiring me to write and spread His Word.

I thank my husband Kent for his unending support and love.

I want to thank my boys, Joel Kent, John Mark, Joshua James, and Joseph David, for filling our home with laughter and bringing spontaneity to our world.

Also, my parents, John and Paula, for their constant encouragement to publish and pursue God's purposes for my life, and my parents-in-law, Kent and Bonnie, for their love of my boys.

Thank you to my grandparents, Sam, Johanna, and Judy, for being such amazing prayer warriors.

Thank you to Carrie, my twin sister, for always hearing my heart.

I want to thank my cousin Leslie for her incredibly helpful suggestions in editing.

Thank you to all my family, for your joy that you bring me.

Thanks to my friends for always believing in my dreams. Thank you also to my friends that have shared with me your heartache from divorce; I have seen God's grace in your lives.

Thank you to all our American soldiers for your service to our country.

I also want to thank Tate Publishing for providing me with the opportunity to publish with a Christian message.

God bless you, the reader for sharing your time with me. I hope you enjoy the book!

Prologue

The hot air gestured at my arms and face, perhaps in an attempt to awaken me from the numbness I felt as my mom and I walked out of the courthouse toward her car. The black asphalt had baked all morning and seemed to move on its own in a steamy mirage.

"Where's your car?" I asked wearily, only too ready to leave this place and its negative memories.

"It's over there, by the tree," Mom said as she pointed to a scrubby tree that sprouted a small bit of coverage from its branches over her navy blue sedan.

My legs worked on their own as my mind mingled with regret. *I'm divorced.* My mouth was dry and bitter tasting. My internal wanderings had made me feel teary and plagued with sadness. I tried to swallow my grief as the lump in my throat grew larger.

We had reached the car and my hand lifted the door handle without really seeing it. I sat down, relieved that I was in the car. Mom had turned the air-conditioner on full blast, and I vaguely realized that she had spoken to me.

"Miranda, I have something for you, if I can find it," my mom said in her heavy New Orleans accent as she reached into her large cavernous purse and handed me a white envelope. "Dawlin', here is a gift you deserve after all that you've been through."

My eyes briefly scanned the contents. "An itinerary for a cruise?" I said, momentarily stunned.

"Now, we are going to have a nice time and not talk about what's-his-face ever again!"

"That might be impossible, considering that he is the father of my children, but a three-day hiatus may be an adequate break from norm—"

"We also won't be using the word 'normal' ever again in our vocabulary, as far as I'm concerned," Mom said in a sassy tone as she backed out of the parking space with a jerk and aimed the car down Colorado Boulevard toward my house.

"True, that word is off the books. I promise!"

"Good, now I know its short notice, but I wanted it to be a surprise. So we are flying out on Friday to Florida, then traveling by taxi to the port where we embark."

"Sounds like you have this all planned out," I said with relief. I truly couldn't think anymore after all I had been through today since leaving court.

"I even will come over and help you pack."

"Thanks, Mom, but I think I can handle it."

"All right, now don't worry about the kids. Papa has them while we are gone. Who knows what they will eat while we are at sea. But I'm sure it will be filling," she said with a wink.

"I'm positive they will survive. I taught them that if nothing else."

"Now, dawlin', don't belittle yourself. Those kids know unconditional love, laughter, and spontaneity because of you. Most of all, they know God. Why, I believe you have had them in church the very week they were born—both of them."

I laughed. "Really, they were always in church, since I was going before they were born."

"Well, now see. It's true, you are a perfect mother."

"Not perfect, but a mom who loves them and has learned, the hard way, that my ultimate value comes from the King Himself."

"The King of kings and the Lord of lords. Yes, you are His child and mine, dawlin' girl. Now you will not believe what he has planned for you in your future. Why I believe that God Himself is smiling right now."

"You do?"

"I do with all my Southern, Louisianan being…and you know that's a powerful thing!" she said as she pulled into my driveway.

"Thanks for dropping me off. I'll see you Friday," I said with a tight squeeze around my mom, not wanting to let go.

"See you then."

I was packed, had hugged the kids for the millionth time, and was finally sitting on the plane next to my mom.

"My head," I groaned.

"You've been through it, and your body is worn-out." She caught the eye of a flight attendant and waved her down. "Miss, can you bring my daughter some water and hot towels?"

"She might have been busy, Mom," I said, feeling a twinge of guilt as I watched the attendant weave down the aisle.

"Never too busy to help, I'm sure," she said as she received the towels and water bottles.

I had to admit, being mothered was a balm for me. Slightly suffocating, but a balm to my wounded heart.

"Now, just rest here until we land," she said and placed the towel on my head with a tender hand.

The rest of the day was a blur of grabbing our luggage, piling into a smelly cab, getting dropped off near the gangplank, standing in long lines before boarding, and then dining in an open-air restaurant aboard the ship.

Once we were settled in our deluxe stateroom, I lay down. Mom shut the curtains over the window that overlooked what would hopefully be the sea in a few hours.

"Sleep, and I'll wake you for dinner."

What Mom did for the next twenty-four hours, I still don't know. I know she came in at some point and dozed for a while. I woke up around 1:00 p.m. the next day.

"What in the world?"

Mom slowly opened the blinds, and I stared out at the lively green and indigo layered waves. White caps sent spray into the air as endless watery hills dipped the cruise ship from valley to valley. I was spell-bound by the view.

"After lunch, let's see some sights around the ship today," Mom said, stepping outside to admire the view from the balcony.

"Splendid!" I said agreeably.

After I showered in the doll-house–sized space, I emerged clean and refreshed. We ate a ridiculous amount of fresh fruit, salad, and shish kebabs and headed to the ship's interior map. Mom and I perused the activities that were available on the main deck.

"Do you want to swim today or try something daring?" Mom turned to me with her brows arched in question.

"Rock wall climbing. What is that?" I asked uncertainly.

"Let's go see!"

Before I knew it, I was in line for my gear. I tilted my head back and looked up at the height of the massive wall. *What was I thinking? A forty-five-foot climbing wall?*

An Aussie named Lochlan gave me some instructions while he checked my harness. "You'll find various handholds along the vertical wall. Some are small called crimps. Those are narrow with a bit of room for your fingertips. Others are 'slopers.' They are slanted, and you grasp them with an open-handed hold. The most uncomplicated hold is a 'jug.' They are large and easily identifiable along your route. If you get washer-board legs, just take the tension off your shaking legs by changing position of your heels. Also, remember to flatten your body, arching your back slightly and keep your knees pointing outward all the way up," he said as he demonstrated, bouncing his knees up and down. "All set, now just start climbing."

"Here I go." I reached for the highest, resin-mounted handhold, placed my foot on the lowest rung, and began to climb in a somewhat splayed fashion. I stepped from one foothold to another, always grabbing the closest handholds.

About halfway up, I looked down. My hands were sweating, and my legs were like Jell-O. Lochlan controlling the tension in my ropes called encouraging words. "All right up there, you've got it!"

I reached for a small "crimp." My hand slipped, and I fell backward. Swinging out, I spiraled to the left. Lochlan held the tension in the rope, and I didn't fall any further.

"Grab a handhold when I swing you back to the wall."

I grabbed a jug and clung to the wall. I felt plastered to it like a bit of chewed gum.

"You didn't think you were going to make it, did you?" the Aussie said, smiling cockily.

"Uh…I thought I was going to plummet to the ground!" I said, allowing my thoughts to dwell on that possibility.

He laughed at the expression on my face, which was creased in pure dread.

"I've got you secure," he called from below. "You are doing fine. Do you want to keep climbing?"

"Yes," I managed to breathe out.

"Okay, then go when you are ready."

I kept climbing higher, letting my feet push my body up. I tried to stay as flat as possible and push up with my feet. I moved slowly until I saw the bell within reach.

Ding, ding, ding! I rang it hard. I looked back from my precarious position. In the distance was the ship's smoke stack, merrily painted red. Beyond the diagonally strung flags, the ocean stretched around me in a wide, unending wash of blue-green waves. I embraced the wind as it stroked my face. I felt, at that very moment, that God was with me, providing comfort from all my heart-cries.

The sun sent dazzling sparkles across the ocean as I looked to my left. I took a deep breath. It was time to repel down and face the next phase of my life—singleness.

Chapter 1

Two years later
Mountain View, Colorado

My name is Miranda. I'm not cynical, though I really should be after the regret of my past marriage, which left behind a trail of broken promises. There is a belief that we have, that "it's all going to work out, if we just keep holding it together." However, marriage takes two, and I soon realized…I was alone.

Our marriage looked ideal, but Ethan's convenient business trips told another tale when I picked up the details of his affairs. Anger, hurt, depression—you name it, I felt it. I asked myself over and over, why didn't I fit into his fairy tale anymore? When I finally confronted him, he only said, "Miranda, I'm sorry, it's just—you're so normal!"

Normal, I sighed. I don't want to think back to that horrendous time of my life. I peered into the mirror and studied my tired reflection. My brown curly hair jingled in place, and my cocoa-colored eyes stared back at me sleepily. I was average height with skin that could tan when I saw the sun, and my thighs rubbed together if I admitted it. Maybe I was too normal. I wasn't exotic or extremely gifted. Perhaps I was just a basic, run-of-the mill, thirty-year-old woman—not special in the least.

Oh, stop it, Miranda. You have got to stop listening to these lies. Fine, I am determined to never let my guard down about men—again. My stomach churned with angry gulps.

"God, I feel betrayed and…I'm doing it again. I'm believing lies. Lord, help me to center my heart on you. I pray you become my true fairy tale."

Glancing out the window, large raindrops scattered in a misty film. The morning's rain further dampened my desire to get on with my day, so I crawled back into bed. Thunder rolled atop the mountain range, echoing its tall voice along the trees. I felt pensive and remorseful that it was morning. I wanted to blame the rain for its hold on me, but I knew it went deeper. I sunk my head into my pillows and whispered to God. *Oh, Lord, today, tomorrow, this year, for the rest of my life, I want to speak with You as Your daughter. If not, I think I'll go crazy. So I want talk to You, tell you things that are going on. Father, you know me, on the inside. My secret battles to be strong and not be overcome by cynicism. I want my life to be guided by You. I've always dreamed of a storybook ending for my life. Since I don't know of all your plans, help me to listen and trust You. I'm not a mistake and neither is my life.*

I thought about how God had provided for me as I stared at the creamy white walls of my room. The wooden clapboard house my children and I lived in was older but had good bones. I had bought it, with some help from my parents, after the divorce for a fresh start. Ethan never let us buy a house; we always rented. Now I realize his lack of commitment was a core quality that I somehow had missed when we were dating.

Real wood floors, large windows with a beautiful view, and fireplaces in many of the rooms were the essence of my home. I loved my upstairs bedroom. It was airy with white curtains that hung floor to ceiling and a white, down-filled comforter on my golden oak, four-poster bed. The windows captured my eyes when I saw the view. Mountain ranges, dipped in clingy cotton anchored against gray-blue skies, held my attention.

The rolling thunder shook the windows slightly and knocked me into action. I pounced my socked feet onto the floor, throwing my covers back almost symbolically on my sour mood and padded back into my bathroom, which I had painted chartreuse when I'd first moved in.

There was also light celery-colored curtains, which accented the window and bath. I couldn't afford to truly remodel so I accepted the avocado-colored sink, which was a throwback from the 1970s. The whole house was a mish-mosh of different eras. In the end, with a fresh coat of paint and some furniture that people had donated, the house had come together. I knew that God, being a master decorator, had provided once again.

I had so much to be thankful for…my children, my job…this view! I glanced out the bathroom window where a jagged mountain peak majestically etched the clouds and dictated the smoky, dripping sky around it.

Thank you, God. You are so full of peace, I can feel it. Your Word says in Psalm 30:5, "Weeping may stay for the night, but rejoicing comes in the morning." Help me to remember that. I will make it through this day without negativity haunting me. I clenched my fist in defiance. *Guess what I think? Normal looks okay!*

I dabbed on my favorite lip gloss and spritzed my hair with shine spray. *In fact*—I shook my coppery curls confidently—*normal looks great!*

As I stomped downstairs determinedly, I repeated my marching orders, *I will have peace and joy from God!*

"Kids, we have to go!" I scrambled, as usual, to get my seven-year-old daughter, Becca, and my ten-year-old son, Ruston, into our cobalt blue Rubicon Jeep and on time for anything. "We have to get to school, and I can't be late for work!"

"We know!" they responded in unison.

Despite their confidence, it was always a challenge to get out of the house with shoes, lunches, and semi-matching, clean clothes.

"Do you have your shoes on?"

Becca, with her soft brown hair pulled back into pigtails, grinned at me. "Yes, *I do.*" She probably remembered only too well a few weeks ago when Ruston got to school and had no socks or shoes on.

"I have mine on now," Ruston sleepily spoke up, hand-combing his blondish-brownish hair. He was not a morning person, hence the lack of footwear previously.

During the drive to school, I prayed with each of them to ask that God would give them a great day. I dropped the kids off with a hug and kiss.

"Bye-bye, I love you!"

"We love you too!" they said, shooting me lopsided smiles and jumping out of the Jeep onto the curb.

Both kids were tall and would probably tower over me eventually. Becca was the enthusiastic one who could bring a smile to anyone. Ruston was athletic, and though he occasionally was moody and had a know-it-all attitude, he had matured over the past two years. He had turned his sadness from the divorce into a protective attitude toward Becca. Even though I was proud of him, I had to make sure that he stayed a kid; it was a balance.

Whether or not it was a good thing, Ruston and Becca were the only reasons for my ex and I to keep talking. He tried to be a good father to them…when it was convenient. The children saw Ethan on some weekends and holidays, but their life was with me. They had good friends here, their grandparents lived here, and they had lots of activities. Being involved at church also provided some outreach and support for them as well as for myself.

I never could have made it these past two years if it hadn't been for Carrie and Scott. We went to the same church, worked together, and most importantly, Carrie was my best friend and was married to Scott. I had known Carrie my entire life.

Carrie and I grew up together. Since grade school, we complemented each other. Her chestnut-colored, board-straight hair always looked flawless, especially against my jumble of curls. Carrie was tall, slender, and had the endearing quality of listening to all my woes. She was slightly more cautious than I, though my adventurous streak usually involved her in some escapade. I remember one time as children when we opened a "store" on our street, complete with a table from my bedroom. We propped up various toys from our houses that we wanted to sell, mostly old Mardi Gras throws, like stuffed animals and plastic knickknacks. We thought we'd made a lot of money when someone gave us a whole quarter! Together we lingered through childhood, exploring the possibilities of life through the eyes of children. I guess it shouldn't have surprised me that we eventually worked together once we were adults.

When Ethan and I divorced, Carrie and Scott offered me a job. Scott and Carrie owned a coffee shop called *Bean Me Up*. It was a popular Trekkie-themed coffee joint with a modern vibe. We worked out a schedule that still allowed me to have time with my kids. Some shifts were longer than others, but I had my mom and dad to help with the kids when I needed to work late.

"Hi, Carrie!" I said as I ran through the back door of the coffee shop.

"Good morning to you, Miranda! Right on time!" she said, winking at me as she tucked her dark brown her behind her ear.

"Oh, you know, always a miracle just getting out of the house!" I replied as I walked behind the counter joining Carrie.

The coffee shop had black walnut tables on stainless steel bases, comfy square chairs, and deep booths. The color scheme was gray, chocolate brown, and cream. Futuristic light fixtures dotted the ceiling, cascading light for reading and relaxing. I quickly tied on my apron, and before I knew it, had rushed through orders of five lattes, two large black coffees, a blended caramel with whip, and a cappuccino with two double shots.

The customers were a mixture of young, old, in a hurry, and "take-your-time-sweetie!" We saw young people from the local community college, lawyers, schoolteachers, physical therapists, and retirees. Everyone loved coming into Bean Me Up. You didn't have to be a Trekkie fan to like this place. The coffee was amazing, and the tray of cinnamon rolls was nearly always empty.

"Miranda, can you manage the front for a few minutes?" Carrie asked as she slipped into her office behind the kitchen. "I have to get some ordering done."

"Sure thing!"

I loved the fact that I could do anything to help out Scott and Carrie. Truly, while God was my absolute, unchanging rock, my mom and dad and my friends Scott and Carrie were my earthly rocks that kept me sane! I didn't know what I would have done without them during the whole divorce trial.

By 11:00 a.m., the busyness slacked up a little. I sprayed and wiped tables; organized the sugar, cinnamon, stirrers, and napkins at the self-serving station; and brewed fresh pots of our house blend and the day's special—Amaretto Dream.

Around 3:00 p.m., we started our "need-a-pick-me-up" time. Frozen, blended, and iced coffees were popular during those hours. Our Crazy Caramel and Mocha Mixed Up frozen coffees were by far the favorites.

"What can I get you? I asked as two guys stepped up to the counter.

"Two large black coffees to-go," one of them replied in a gruff, slightly accented English.

"Can I tempt you with one of our fruit salads or some muffins?" I asked, offering him a smile.

"No, just the coffee, and we're in a hurry," the taller man grumbled, impatient with life.

Both sets of eyes looked piercing, dark, and intense. I looked down, breaking their steely gaze. I noticed one of them kept his hands balled in his pockets, like he was holding something and the other shifted his feet.

"Oh, sure, no problem," I replied.

I filled two red insulated cups and sealed the lids on top. After I handed the men their drinks, they paid and left rapidly. I wasn't offended by their need to hurry. In fact, I prided myself on my ability to get customers in and out as speedily as possible. But their demeanor had bothered me. I was left with a sort-of nervous relief when they were gone.

The evening shift girls arrived at 3:30 p.m., and I clocked out. Carrie gave me a quick hug before I left. She would be leaving soon after she filled in the college girls with their duties for the night. Scott usually came by each evening to help lock up and collect the money from the register. They had a good system worked out. Scott was the accountant and handled all the taxes, banking, license, and payroll. Carrie was really good with PR, advertising, and of course, people! She interviewed the coffee baristas and dealt with any communication or problems between the employees. Carrie had a thoughtful demeanor and discretion, which came from the Holy Spirit. Scott valued these characteristics in Carrie and stepped in only when it was needed.

Humming to myself as I navigated my Jeep toward the school, I mentally ran down a to-do list. Since the weather was getting cooler, I would have to pull down the kids' winter clothes from the attic. Supper was a predictable chore on the list, but what was less obvious was what we would be having. I thought I could remember some frozen chicken that needed to come out of the freezer. I would love to believe that I was this amazing chef. Flambé this and sauce-a-la-that. That, of course, would be outright lies. I have regularly burned things as I multitasked by unloading the dishwasher and sautéed some dinner concoction simultaneously.

Just yesterday, I had warmed some frozen-mini-pizza-pocket-things, and they all got stuck to the bottom of the pan. I served the ones that were only smudged to the kids and scraped the hard, black crust off mine. They broke apart, but the insides were pretty good.

At least I had mastered waffles, but it was probably the syrup that saved them. My skill at blending things was acceptable. Strawberry-mango smoothies were a favorite around our house.

Unfortunately, my biggest problem was my inability to follow directions, and cookbooks were just *so* factual. I would look at a recipe, especially the pictures, write down the ingredients, and then wonder if it was really worth it. The cost alone of groceries was so high. If I have to buy all the ingredients for the recipe and then it really didn't taste that good…I guess I don't want to be disappointed. My track record with cooking was a little hard to swallow.

Hopefully, Ruston and Becca didn't really care that much about whether I burnt pizza, because I loved them and they knew it. As I pulled into the parking lot, I tapped my fingers on the steering wheel, feeling just as excited as I did every day to see them and hug the life out of them.

Ruston ran track until around 4:00 p.m., and Becca had her art class. I was thankful the school had so many after-school options. Becca also took ballet on Thursday nights at a quaint little studio called The Slipper. With her recitals and Ruston's track meets on top of their regular homework, we kept pretty busy during the week. However, I couldn't complain, and there were always adventures on Saturday and church on Sunday to look forward to.

I parked the Jeep and went inside the school. The halls felt quiet until I entered Becca's well-lit art room. The exuberant walls painted in yellow greeted me before Becca saw me.

"Hi, sweetie!" I said, giving her a hug.

"Hi, Mom! Look at this!" She displayed a beautiful, carefully drawn picture of a house, which was clipped to her easel. "It's our house!" she spoke proudly. "See the brown roof and the green shutters? I tried to draw a swing on the front porch, but it kind of squished together."

"I love it! Of course I see our house. Hey, you even got the birds' nest in the tree from the front yard," I said.

"Mrs. Colvin?" Becca's art teacher stepped forward.

"Hi, Mrs. Flayten, please, call me Miranda."

I disliked that I was so sensitive to my last name, but it wasn't who I was anymore. Ethan and I had been divorced for two years. Regrettably, I still had his last name due to a flaw in the divorce papers.

"Oh yes, of course, dear. Becca is doing wonderfully and so enthusiastic!" Her tinkly earrings clanked as she spoke. "Becca and all the students will be featured in a fall art show located in the town library. I believe every child should be appreciated like the fine artists that they are!" Her colorful scarf and flowy skirt swayed to a dramatic finish.

"Thank you so much for all your effort with Becca. She truly seems to be enjoying the class."

"She is a pleasure to teach, simply a joy!" Mrs. Flayten said.

"Wonderful. God has blessed me with a special girl!" I said, pulling Becca close to my side. "See you tomorrow."

Becca and I headed down the hall toward the back of the school. "Well, should we go get your brother? I asked mischievously.

"No. Let's leave him with the rest of those smelly boys at the field!" Becca said with a giggle.

"True. He will need a shower. But I think that we should pick him up anyway," I said, tucking my hand in Becca's.

When we entered the track and football field, I spotted Ruston and the rest of the guys listening attentively to the coach. Even though this was a public school, Coach Jack was actually a Christian and even went to the same church as we did. Since Ethan wasn't really in his son's life anymore, Ruston needed good role models, and I was thankful that Coach Jack was a kind man who loved the Lord and saw athleticism as a true ministry.

Becca and I waited by the stands until the boys broke up with a resounding clap and shout of "Win!"

"Hi, Ruston! Are you ready?" I asked as Ruston jogged over to us with a smile.

"Yeah, Coach wore us out today, but I feel ready for our next competition. He really encouraged us. He even quoted my favorite scripture verse. 'They that wait upon the Lord shall renew their strength. They shall run and not be weary. They shall walk and not faint.'"

I smiled as Ruston finished reciting the verse. Last year, he had pinned up in his room a poster of a runner with that verse on the bottom.

"I hope he doesn't get in trouble quoting scripture like that," I said.

Ruston replied confidently, "Nah, Coach always tells us to not be afraid of speaking God's Word. He even quotes Spurgeon saying something like, 'The Word of God is like a lion, all you have to do is let it out of its cage, and it will take care of itself.' The gospel will defend itself if we let it."

"Good word, Ruston," I said as I hugged him.

As we headed back to the car, I added, "I think I needed to hear that. If I say, 'God bless you' to someone, I feel I have witnessed to them. But God may desire more than that. I know I have been under conviction lately. Instead of being afraid of what to say, I should quote a scripture verse."

"What verse would you say, Mom?" Becca asked.

"Um, how about saying to the person, 'Can I share one of my favorite verses with you?' If they say 'yes,' then I would recite Romans 6:23, 'For the wages of sin is death, but the free gift of God is eternal life in Christ Jesus our Lord.'"

On the drive home, we all chattered about our day. When we got home, Ruston got in the shower, Becca went to her room to play, and I faced the dreaded chicken in the freezer.

"Okay, chicken, it's you or me."

I dropped the chicken breasts into a bowl of hot water and called my mom.

"Hello, Mom," I said when she picked up the phone. "Can you help me with a 'chicky' situation?"

Her laughter rang out. "Oh, honey, *what* are you trying to cook?"

"How do you make that Parmesan chicken dish that the kids love?" I asked.

"Do you have butter, eggs, milk, Parmesan, and Italian bread crumbs?" Mom asked.

"Let me look…" I said, poking through the fridge and the pantry. "Yes! Yes, I do."

Mom began, "Get out two bowls. Crack a few eggs in a bowl and pour some milk on top. Then stir together."

Tucking the phone against my shoulder, I fished some bowls out of the dishwasher. "Wait, should I measure something?" I asked.

"You can, but will you?" she asked dubiously.

"You're right. I probably won't. Give me a sec," I said as I began mixing ingredients. "Okay, so I have my eggs and milk whisked together."

Mom continued her instructions. "In your second bowl, dump half the can of Italian breadcrumbs and half the can of Parmesan cheese together. Stir that up. In the microwave, melt a stick of butter in a bowl. Then dredge the chicken."

"Wait—what's 'dredge'?" I asked curiously.

"You know, swish and dip the chicken in the egg, then roll it in the breadcrumb-Parmesan mixture. Got it?"

"Yeah, I think so."

"Okay, now lay the chicken strips in a casserole pan. Once you have dipped all the chicken, pour the melted butter over it and cover with foil. Bake for one hour at 350 degrees or until the chicken is no longer pink on the inside." She laughed. "It's going to be great, dawlin'. Just keep trying and you will turn out to be a great cook! Now, how are my babies, and when am I going to see them?"

27

I filled her in on the kids' recent events and made some plans for when she could see them, as I prepared the chicken and popped it in the oven. Since I knew I was working late twice this week, my parents could pick up the kids from school on those days.

"You know, next Saturday my hiking club is going to meet. We leave so early. Maybe the kids could spend the night next Friday with y'all?"

"Honey, that sounds wonderful. Your dad and I would love for them to come!"

"Well, I better go and check on that chicken. Love you, Mom!"

"You too, Miranda. Hug the kids from us and know that we pray for you every day!"

"Thanks, Mom. I needed to hear that," I said, feeling tender.

To my relief, the chicken came out unburned, and the kids were ecstatic.

"Parmesan chicken and a salad? Mom, do this again!" Ruston said enthusiastically.

"Yeah, Mom. This is awesome!" Becca chimed in.

"So there is hope for me yet. You see we can all learn something new." I gave them a happy grin. "Just like in school, homework time!"

Both kids groaned.

"Let's just get it done and then we can relax a little bit before bed," I said, trying to sound positive.

This was one of those times when I wished for a second pair of hands. Pushing through after a long day by myself was arduous. I said a prayer to God in my heart and felt His peace and joy.

"Thank you, God!"

"What did you say, Mom?" Ruston asked.

"I was just thanking God for you both. You know that both of you are big blessings."

Becca jumped up from the table. "Did you say 'big blessings'?"

Without waiting for an answer, she grabbed a pillow from the couch and pounced on me. Ruston jumped up and threw a pillow onto me too.

Now it was war!

"Pillow power!" I yelled.

We ran around the living room, diving under the table and ducking into doorways. It was a "pure fun" moment. We all needed it.

"Whew! That was hilarious!" I said after all pillows had been replaced to their proper couches. "Okay, let's finish up homework and get ready for bed."

The kids worked diligently as I finished cleaning the kitchen. While Ruston and Becca got ready for bed, I stepped onto the porch. The evening was beginning to spread over the mountains. I could hear the crickets speaking to each other. I breathed deeply, completing a full breath. I needed to do that more often.

"Father, I just want to breathe in your love and thank you for who you are. I pray I will be the fragrance of Christ to those who meet me. Let me be a vessel of love and help me not be afraid to witness about you. I love you, God."

I took another moment to survey the mountains as the sun dipped into the sky's deepening silken folds.

Chapter 2

The morning came in a triumphant blast of cool air. October was here. I reached for my phone calendar and thumbed through the days. Today was going to be a long one. I was scheduled to come in at ten this morning and work until a little after six. Carrie sometimes needed a later shift from me when the college girls had exams. My mom and dad would pick the kids up from school. While I held my phone, I read over a devotional from an app I had recently downloaded:

Lady Liberty speaks her truth to America with:

The New Colossus by Emma Lazarus

"Keep, ancient lands, your storied pomp!" cries she
With silent lips. "Give me your tired, your poor,
Your huddled masses yearning to breathe free,
The wretched refuse of your teeming shore.
Send these, the homeless, tempest-tost to me,
I lift my lamp beside the golden door!

Jesus speaks to us: "Come to me, all you who are weary and burdened, and I will give you rest" (Matthew 11:23).

Though we live in a beautiful and free America, we still have this old world pulling at our lives and hearts. We all look for the answers to our problems through whatever means we gain or can tangibly see. Some people may seemingly have so many things to make them happy, yet they are still overwhelmed and unhappy. We may think that a perfect house, perfect spouse, angel kids, and all the money we could ever use could, somehow, fill our void.

However, we know that God is the one with the ultimate rest and peace. He is our void filler and life giver.

Amen to that! I thought. Sometimes I believed if only the endless supply of to-be-fixed items at our house like the leaking washing machine, the broken disposal, the fading paint on the house, and the pile of clothes that needed to be folded could all be resolved, I would be satisfied. I would feel content and not as embarrassed about my inability to do everything! I really needed to accept God's pure love for me and see Him as the One that gives me rest. His view of me is based on perfect love. So much love for me that he sent His Son Jesus to die on the cross for my sins. Then Jesus conquered death and rose again on the third day. I am not trusting in a god…I am trusting in *the* God who lives in victory eternally! Maybe, I can live in victory too!

"I love you, God!" I said aloud. I felt His love linger around me and grew content. It was a good feeling!

I better get into high gear. I heard the kids downstairs moving around.

"Mom, we are out of cereal!"

"Oh no, let me make some muffins," I called out as I came down the stairs. I had bought some muffin mixes that just needed milk. We are probably going to be hungry. I mused, so I will combine the honey bran with the apple cinnamon pouch. How much milk? I read the back and it stated one-third cup of milk for one and two-thirds for another. I grabbed the measuring cup, poured some milk in it, dumped it into the bowl, and stirred.

"Oh great!" I muttered sarcastically. It looked all liquidy. I think I mismeasured my milk. "All right, you muffins, just wait!" I scooped in several tablespoons of flour until it looked more lumpy and thick. Becca helped grease the muffin pans. Ruston spooned some sugar on the top of each muffin. "Walah, muffins—you are going to taste good!" I said as I put the tray in the preheated oven.

"Uh, Mom, you're talking to the food again," Ruston scolded slightly.

"Hey, some people talk to their plants, I talk to the food. It can't hurt!" I replied with a shrug and smiled.

Becca giggled. The muffins rose up in the pan and crusted over with the sugar topping. "Mmmm. These are delicious. Ms. Carrie is going to want your recipe for Bean Me Up!" Becca said as we ate.

"Maybe if you wrote the recipe down, you could add the correct amount of milk," Ruston said amused with himself.

"Yes, I think I will. But you know, not everybody has a math-brain like you! That's why doing great in school is so important!" I zinged back at him, laughing!

"Oh, Mom!" Ruston ducked his head into my arms as I hugged him tight. We were a team and a family for better or for worse.

I dropped the kids off at school and went to the store before heading to work. I picked up some cereal and oatmeal for breakfast options and some miscellaneous groceries. Hopefully, that would last a couple of days until payday.

"Good morning, Scott!" I said breezily as I came into work. "Is Carrie here this morning?" "Actually, the twins were sick last night. So she stayed home with them today."

The twins, Casey and Stacey, were three years old. A boy and a girl with wheat-colored hair. Carrie tried to get pregnant for years before they finally conceived. The twins were a double miracle! "Oh, I am sorry to hear that. I will be praying. How was the morning rush?" I asked.

"Busy and the milk steamer is on the blink. So hold the button down the whole time when you are using it," Scott said, looking at me with hazel eyes that were framed by his modern black glasses.

"I gotcha," I said, nodding.

Getting into a rhythm, I moved busily through the day. I enjoyed being a coffee barista. I felt like God used my love of people in a unique way. An encouraging word, smile, and maybe someday…a verse I could share! Around 3:00 p.m., those two moody guys that had bought coffees yesterday stopped in. They ordered the same black coffee, but for here. I placed two oversized cups filled with steamy coffee in front of them while they paid. I was pleasant but guarded after our last conversation. I glanced at them when they sat down in a corner booth. Their conversation seemed heated but low. One man plunked some items from his pockets on the table. He separated the items in a pattern. He began pointing to his keys, the cups of coffee, some papers, and other smallish, flat pieces. Each item seemed to represent something. I saw one of them shake a hand at the other, indicating a negative response. The man on the right unfolded a laptop and typed rapidly. The other guy tapped the screen once and nodded. Overhearing a word that sounded familiar, I stayed still for a moment, but I couldn't quite make it out. When some of the college students came in, the orders for Mocha Mixed Up and Caramel Crazy kept me busy with the blender for a while. They were laughing and bantering back and forth about various philosophies and discussions of friends.

An hour later, the two guys got up from their table as the college students left. I headed over to the tables with some cleaning solution and towels. I noticed some napkins on the floor, where the two men had sat. As I picked them up, a thumb drive fell onto the floor.

"Oh no. Those guys must have dropped this."

I ran out to the parking lot, but they were already gone. I stuck it in my brown apron pocket, thinking I would see them soon.

"Just missed them," I said slightly out of breath as I walked back through the front door.

Scott looked up from the counter and said, "Did somebody forget their cell phone again?"

"No, a thumb drive. I wonder what's on it. They seemed pretty tense while they were here. I am curious to know what they are working on."

"You know what Carrie would say, if she heard you now?" Scott said, shaking his index finger at me in mock accusation.

"I know, I know, 'Keep your nose out of trouble and trouble won't nose around you!'"

"Do you want to put it in the lost-and-found crate?" Scott asked, reaching for it under the counter.

"No, I think I will keep it with me for safekeeping, I don't want anything to spill on it," I replied as I finished wiping the tables.

A few minutes later, I looked around at Scott and saw him adjusting the digital menu above our heads. Its high-def pixels clearly indicated the menu choices. Chrome and low lights surrounded the frame.

"So my kids wanted to tell Carrie about the new muffins we created this morning."

"Yeah, what was that?" Scott asked as he stepped down from the step stool.

"Honey, bran, apple, cinnamon," I said

"You will have to run a taste test with Carrie, but sounds good!" Scott replied with an interested look as he tapped his auburn goatee.

I chuckled as I told him of our *creativity* for the morning. "So speaking of new menu items. Did you add in the new turkey and smoked cheese filo pastry?"

"Yes, the updated menu has just been uploaded…it's coming up right now," Scott observed as the readout clarified.

"Cool! That looks amazing. Who would have thought your Trekkie *obsession* and Carrie's coffee *love* would have conspired so well together?" I stated.

"All I can say is, "It's a God thing, and He is good. He knows what He is doing. Which is a really great thing, since I don't have all the know-how. Especially with carpentry," Scott said with a twinkle in his eye. We smiled as we remembered the cradles Scott tried to build before the twins were born. Let's just say, they lacked functionality.

"I guess I am not surprised that Jesus was a terrific carpenter. He can put the pieces of our lives back together and make it all fit. He uses our mistakes, our failures, and even our love for one another to bring about a beautiful masterpiece called... life," Scott said with feelings.

"Absolutely! I am a living testimony of seeing Jesus put my life back together," I said.

Scott continued, "In reference to carpentry, one day, I'd like to expand this place even more. The second floor of this building may be coming up for lease soon. Wouldn't it be neat to add an interior elevator called a transporter? Moms with kids in strollers and people with wheelchairs could easily glide in and transport to an upper balcony set with tables and couches that overlooked the mountains and the busy street below. We could have Wi-Fi and outlets up there too so the people that had laptops could have more access points. Maybe even a youth or college group could reserve that area for Bible studies!"

"Scott, that does sound amazing! Keep that dream alive, I think it would be an incredible asset to *Bean Me Up*!"

It was Ethan's weekend to take the kids. He came down for one of Ruston's track meets. Ruston did amazing, with his team placing first in the relay. Afterward, Ethan, who was lithe and agile, which he maintained through a gym membership, loaded up Becca, Ruston, and all the kids' luggage into his red Ferrari sports car.

"Do you all fit?" I asked. Becca looked pretty snug in the back.

"Sure, I'm fine!" Becca replied, smiling. I had hugged the kids a few minutes ago so all that was left was to give some final instructions to Ethan. Ethan checked his Rolex, set off by his designer azure shirt, and cocked his gelled blond head at me, as his blue eyes glazed over.

Waving good-bye, I felt a surge of maternal instincts threaten to overwhelm me. Tears started to roll down my cheeks. *Stop feeling sad*, I whispered to myself. I knew that they were safe and well cared for. I was even a little happy that they could spend time with their dad. Ethan lived an hour away in the big city of Salix. Ruston texted me with the ecstatic news that they were going to a hockey game that night. Later that evening, he sent me a picture of them at the game, which included his dad's newest cheerleader girlfriend.

The caption read, "She seems nice, but I can't remember her name."

Not that it mattered that much to me. Rarely, has his "relationships" lasted very long. I prayed for the children's physical and spiritual protection. I would be glad when they came home on Sunday evening.

Saturday morning came early as I cleaned, organized, and ran errands. I texted Carrie that I needed a girls' night out. Carrie was totally pumped and came up with the great idea of camping. Maybe I was rubbing off on Carrie regarding adventures. Or perhaps, it was just our need to fight through a man's world, so I consented on one condition—Carrie would do the cooking. Scott was amused at the idea of Carrie camping, but he agreed to watch their kids and planned a night with them.

By 2:00 p.m., we arrived in the nearby National Park in my Jeep and set up camp.

"Do the tent rods go this way?" Carrie asked.

"I guess," I responded. We struggled with the crisscross pattern of the rods, tucking the ends into the thin, coated, polyester sleeves positioned at the four corners of the tent.

"Bring it up," I said, attempting to hoist one side of the tent. It was comical as we anchored the tent pegs down into the ground, trying to secure the lines of the tent. The tent kept bending and twisting in opposite directions.

"Whew!" Carrie said.

"Does it look okay?" I asked.

Carrie put her hands on her hip and surveyed our makeshift palace. "Amazing!" she said, laughing. We high-fived with a shout of "Girl power!"

We were probably a little too proud of our castle.

We built a fire in the fire ring and relaxed with some hot chocolate that Carrie brought in a thermos. We had eaten a tasty supper of grilled hamburgers that Carrie had cooked on the outdoor grill at our site.

"Success! No kids, no men, just best friends enjoying the stars and listening to nighttime nature sounds," I said with a satisfied sigh.

Though we worked together, went to the same church, and spent days of our childhood in sync with one another…we never ran out of things to talk about. Oh sure, we needed our space too, from time to time, but friendships like this were one in a trillion.

"I'm *exhausted*," I said dramatically as I thought back to my whirlwind morning. Carrie agreed. As a mother of twins, "exhaustion" was a word she understood. I turned down the knob on the lantern and said gruffly, "Lights out."

Carrie giggled and said, "Just like when our moms used to tell us when we stayed up too late during our never-ending sleepovers." We laughed with the memory and eventually settled down into our somewhat comfortable sleeping bags.

By three in the morning, rain was pounding our tent with an unrelenting force. Water leaked into all four sides of our temporary abode like a little moat surrounding a castle. Only, we were in the middle of it. My sleeping bag was drenched because it had absorbed the water from the walls of the tent. Our canopy that had supposedly added extra shade over the top of the tent was tugging violently at its tent pegs. The wind blew down one side, tipping the canopy's collected water down the outer tent walls. This sent splashes of rainwater through the nets that formed windows on each side of the tent.

"I'm not laughing right now," I said as I felt around for my flashlight.

"I'm soaked and cold," Carrie said with a grimace.

"So much for the greatest girls' night out ever!" I said hopelessly, wiping my wet legs off with my hands.

Rain slammed our tent for two more hours. We sat hunched together, trying to stay warm. Five in the morning came none too soon. It was still dark outside, but the cold, icy rain had calmed to a drizzle. I saw some headlights as a large vehicle stopped in front of our campsite. I could see a park ranger, with a dripping hat through the wet net of our "window," getting out of his SUV and walking over.

"You campers all right?" he asked.

"We survived," I said, muffled by the insides of the tent. Glumly, we got out of the tent to survey the damage.

"So much for girl power," pointing with my flashlight to our half-drowned tent.

"Well, some tents were blown down completely. In fact, a group of guys at 5E rolled down the hill in their tent." the ranger said, wringing his hands slightly and looking concerned.

"Maybe we should be thankful for God power!" Carrie said wisely.

I finally waved my flashlight in the ranger's direction and noticed his clean-cut face and appearance. I felt a little quiver run down my back. Then I glanced down at my wet, running pants, rolled up to my knees, and could only imagine what my face looked like. A large raindrop dripped on my head and my wet hair slapped a little sense into me.

I spoke up. "Well, thanks for checking up on us." I said non-nonchalantly. I bumped Carrie's elbow and tried to silently plead something.

"Oh, could you give us a hand for a sec?" she asked.

I blinked twice, swiping rain off my ponytail.

"We could really use the help taking down the wet tent—if you don't mind," she added as I cocked my head to one side.

"Sure, ladies. I'll be happy to." With sure hands, he knelt down in the watery moat and easily pulled up the tent pegs.

"You did a nice job of securing your tent," the park ranger said, glancing around.

Carrie handed me a wet rope as I nodded stupidly. I tugged the rope until it pulled off the canopy.

Since the sun shelter was already half down and filled with water, it came down with a splash on my soaked shoes. I willed my feet to walk around the tent and began fiddling with a knot on one of the tent rods.

"Here, let me get that for you," he said chivalrously, untying the doubled knot.

"How can we thank you?" Carrie said while I began wringing back my wet ponytail one more time.

"It's no problem, ladies. All part of the job!" With a nod and touch of his hat, he pulled away into his vehicle.

"Ooh, that was nice," Carrie said. I nodded and bit my bottom lip looking a little lovestruck.

The sunrise the next morning out my bedroom window was magnificent—golden yellow exploded with rose and lavender rays. My whole room became prisms of color celebrating off my walls, my bed, and my face. I posted on my Facebook account a snapshot of the morning sun meet and greet with the verse "The heavens declare the glory of God; the skies proclaim the work of His hands." The rest of the verse continued as I read Psalm 19:1–6, "As day after day they pour forth speech; night after night, they display knowledge. There is no speech or language where their voice is not heard. Their voice goes out into all the earth, their words to the ends of the world. In the heavens he has pitched a tent for the sun, which is like a bridegroom coming forth from his pavilion, like a champion rejoicing to run his course. It rises at one end of the heavens and makes its circuit to the other; nothing is hidden from its heat." I truly love my Creator and am amazed at his divine revelation through creation. This world is full of God's touch. Our eyes just have to be open!

The next week flew by. Between church activities, Ruston's track practices, Becca's art and dance classes, homework, and the unlimited supply of dirty laundry…life's ebb and flow felt like a tidal wave. The kids were going to Gramma and Papa's house tonight.

Friday was here! Hallelujah!

I dropped them off, but not before enjoying an amazing dinner that Mom had made. Roast cooked to perfection, buttered carrots, mashed potatoes, and homemade gravy. Her Southern roots were well established. Mom and Dad had retired up here when the kids were little so they could be closer. At least we all had one delicious meal this week. My cooking had taken a turn for the worse in the latter part of the week.

Chapter 3

My alarm on my phone went off at 4:30 a.m. I was to meet my hiking group at the trailhead Yonder Call at 5:00 a.m. The trail was in the center of the National Park, so I had a twenty-minute drive. I basically had ten minutes to jump into my hiking boots, slip on my favorite light green shorts, white T-shirt and warm, brown hoodie, and head out. I had packed a turkey wrap, an apple, some granola bars and refilled my water bottle last night. I said a quick prayer of safety and hopped in my Jeep. With the mountain roads, I was glad that my off-road vehicle gripped the road, even if there was only gravel.

I admit; I was speeding. Everything takes longer than you think and the clock was ticking. The speed limit sign posted was twenty-five miles per hour, but I paid no attention.

"Oh no! Blue lights!" My stomach doubled in a clenched knot. "Why would anyone care how fast I was driving at 5:00 a.m.?" I wondered with annoyance. A forest ranger walked up to my now motionless vehicle.

"Do you know how fast you were driving, ma'am?" he asked sternly.

"Uh, yes officer. I was going about forty, I think."

"Ma'am, you were going forty-five in a twenty-five—in a National Park. I will be writing you a ticket."

I looked incredulously at his vaguely familiar face and noticed his deep green eyes. I was disarmed by his ruggedly handsome looks and my feelings of aggravation went out of me. I managed to reply contritely, "Oh, okay, I'm sorry." After the ticket incident, I drove like a turtle. I muttered audibly to myself, "The sign now says twenty miles per hour, I think I'll go nineteen miles per hour, Mr. Park Ranger."

"That's the park ranger!" I said aloud as I conked my forehead with my right hand several times. It had suddenly dawned on me that he was the ranger who checked up on us after the monsoon. "I can't wait to tell Carrie!" reaching for my phone. "Wait, she would kill me if I sent her a text this time of the morning," I audibly argued with myself. I finally contented myself with the fact that I would see her on Sunday at church, Monday at the latest. We would talk then. "Though I don't know why I even cared. I was not even interested in him or anyone for that matter. He gave me a ticket for goodness sake. Wow. I really am desperate. No, I'm happy and complete." My self-analysis went on for another ten minutes, after which I arrived at the parking lot for the trailhead.

I was late, of course, to the start of the hike. A few stragglers remained unloading their gear or stretching. I got out of the Jeep and walked up to a petite young woman.

"Hi. I'm Miranda!"

"Good morning, I'm Giselle Li. Wow, this is really early! Jerome, why are we here at this time?" she asked as a tall, dark-skinned man with curly black hair strode over with a dazzling smile. "Because you are going to love it so much when you see the sunrise! Plus, this trail is about eight miles round trip, so we are going to need to get a move on. Ready?" he asked both of us.

Giselle and I both smiled at each other and nodded. I could hardly wait to get going. Moving into a natural stride, we started out. I was glad to have my hoodie. It was chilly this morning. I knew I would warm up later in the morning, but right now, the air was crisp and bit into my cheeks.

At a steady clip, we eventually caught up to some of the group. I said hello to a few of my friends. The Mountain Hiking Club was a great way for me to try some new hikes and meet friends. I hoped that maybe I could be a "light" in it as well. The hike was so invigorating and the views rewarded us repeatedly. After the third mile, we ascended to the most strenuous portion of the trail. I dug deep into the toes of my boots and felt my thighs burning as I pushed forward up the steep slant. Higher and higher we climbed until there were less trees, and the sky poured the glittering hues of the morning on our faces. The panorama at the top was brilliant. I could literally see mountains and valleys in every direction. I sat down and drank in the glorious moment. I took a long swig of my water bottle and enjoyed the sunrise. Various hikers were taking pictures, and we took a great group photo together.

Giselle, her boyfriend Jerome, my friends, Lizzy and Rock, and I started down. Our camaraderie was enjoyable and light-hearted as we made our descent. Giselle asked me to take a picture of her against the Colorado blue sky. The wind blew her short, silky, black hair around her face, and she laughed.

"Cute picture!" I said as I snapped the shot. "The view is really amazing from up here. It reminds me of a verse from the Bible that I read yesterday. "The heavens declare the glory of God, the skies proclaim the work of His hands," I said with fervor.

Giselle nodded.

My mind said, *Here is an opportunity to share about Jesus.* Taking a deep breath and prayer, I said, "I have another favorite verse, would you like to hear it?"

Giselle smiled and said, "Sure!"

I began, "Romans 6:23 tells us, 'For the wages of sin is death, but the free gift of God is eternal life in Christ Jesus our Lord.' That verse means because we make mistakes we don't deserve to go to heaven. However, the Good News is that Jesus Christ paid the price for our sin by dying on the cross. Then he conquered death and rose again. All you have to do is give Jesus your heart and life by trusting in Him! Is that something you have done or would like to do?" I asked with a smile.

Giselle blinked tears from her eyes and said, "I have been wanting to know more about God. Jerome and I have been searching for some clues to how our lives could have more meaning. I thought I wasn't good enough. I kept trying to be good, and I kept doing things that I knew I shouldn't. Do you really think God loves me?" Giselle asked tearfully.

"Giselle, God loves you just the way you are. He created you. He knows you in the inner parts of your heart. Though God doesn't like when we sin, He has a plan for our forgiveness. The first part of the plan is Jesus and the cross. The second part of that salvation equation is *us*. If we accept Jesus as Savior, then we accept His righteousness, His pure love and sacrifice, to cover our sins completely," I answered.

"Does everybody go to heaven?" Giselle asked.

"Giselle, you asked a good question. The answer to that question has a hard truth. The Bible says in Matthew 7:13–14, 'Wide is the gate that leads to destruction…and narrow the gate that leads to life…' Though our salvation is not dependent on works that we ourselves contribute, it is absolutely dependent upon Jesus Christ and His perfect sacrifice. He was the lamb that was slain for us.

"Many people imagine a giant scale that we live on." I extended my arms on either side of me and rocked slightly to the left and right. "Some believe that if our good outweighs our bad, then we go to heaven. It sounds great, be nice to everybody, maybe make a mistake or two and all is okay for the pearly gates. Unfortunately, that teaching is not in the Bible. Even in the Old Testament, the first part of the Bible, people had to have a perfect sacrifice to remove sin. Once Jesus came, lived a perfect life, died on the cross, and then rose again on the third day, the need for sacrificing at a temple was over. The temple curtain was torn."

Giselle nodded in understanding.

I closed with these words, "Jesus was the ultimate sacrifice, and it was truly finished on the cross. Jesus paid all the debt for whole world, but we still have to recognize the sender of the gift by accepting Him into our hearts. Imagine the cross is a Christmas tree and at the bottom of the cross is a gorgeous present with your name on it. Giselle, unless you open your heart to receive God's free gift, you don't have eternal life. Does that make sense?"

"You have given me so much to think about. I really had no idea what the Bible said," Giselle said.

"Giselle, would you like to know for certain that if you died today that you could spend eternity in heaven?" I asked, feeling the Spirit encourage me.

"Miranda, I would like to know for certain. Can you help me?" she asked tentatively.

"I would love to!" I said enthusiastically. I prayed with her a short sinner's prayer, recognizing that we all have sinned and that we needed Jesus Christ as Lord and Savior in order to receive an entrance into heaven.

"Repeat after me, Giselle. God, I thank you that you love me. Please forgive me of all my sins, past, present, and future. Please come into my heart and be my Lord (the one in charge of my life) and Savior. I love You. In Jesus' name, amen!"

Giselle and I hugged on the mountain trail overlooking the valley below. I couldn't believe it—Giselle just got saved! We were both so happy.

Giselle and I caught up with our friends and continued hiking down. I was thrilled when Giselle took Jerome's hand, and she shared with him of her new hope in Jesus Christ.

He seemed very happy for her and said to me, "Maybe we can check out your church on Sunday?"

"Of course! I go to God's Mountain View Church. The Sunday's service is at 10:00 a.m."

You couldn't have taken my smile away for a million dollars. Why did I think witnessing had to be so hard? Giselle had been seeking God for a long time. I had the privilege of bringing in the harvest. Luke 10:2 states, "The harvest is plentiful, but the laborers are few."

When I got back to the Jeep, I noticed one of my tires was flat. On further inspection, a few things were knocked around in the car. The glove box was dumped out, and my duffel bag that I kept in the car for emergencies had been spilled out. What was going on? Lizzy was getting into her car when I started to cry.

"What's wrong, girl?" she asked with a concerned face walking over.

"I think someone broke into my car!"

"Uh, you're gonna have to call the police or somethin'."

While the girls from our group came over and gave me a hug, the guys started inspecting my tire. The heavy duty tires on my Jeep were not easily pierced by rocks.

Jerome looked up from the tire and spoke a word that sent chills down my back, "Slashed." "What?" I shouted, looking alarmed.

"Girl, that's freaky," Lizzy said.

"What'd you do?" someone joked.

"Okay, this is serious. Who would do that? I am not mixed up with anything," I asked plaintively.

Jerome pointed to the long indentations around the tire. A knife had to have made those. Two of the guys from our hiking group flagged down a park ranger. He pulled into the parking area, got out, and walked over to our group, which were surrounding my Jeep.

"Fill me in people, what's the trouble. Everyone starting talking at once, until those green eyes spied me. He held up a hand for silence. My mind kicked me with an adrenaline pulse. *Oh great, that's the cute park ranger who gave me the ticket this morning. He's not going to believe this.*

"Well…" my voice came out wobbly. "I came out to the Jeep and the soft top had been ripped open, my stuff had been messed with and my back tire is slashed."

The park ranger looked down at me and his face softened. "Do you have any idea who could have done this?" he asked.

"No, no, I really don't," I said, looking downtrodden.

"All right, I'll file a report and we will notify local police as well. If some kids are doing this, we will catch them," he spoke confidently.

"Thanks," I said as a little smile peaked out of me.

"I'm sorry this happened to you, ma'am. You know that I try to keep this park safe," he replied with a little twinkle in his deep, green eyes.

I bit my lip and nodded with understanding. I'm glad he didn't rat me out to my friends about the speeding ticket.

"He was very courteous and professional, Dad. The park ranger said he would file a report," I said as I spoke to my dad on the phone.

"Honey, these things happen. Kids looking for trouble is probably all it was. Just be safe and bring your belongings in with you from now on."

"Sugar, they might have seen your duffel bag and thought it had something worth stealing," Mom spoke up. Apparently she was on the other phone listening in. She was never one to miss out on any of the action.

In the past, we had laughed over my in-case-of-emergency bag. The bag contained an assortment of backup clothes for the kids and myself, snacks, sunscreen, bug spray, lip balm, flashlight, bear spray, snow chains—anything I might need in an emergency. Mom and Dad always teased me about what I carried in that bag.

"One day, the kitchen sink will pop out of that big bag!" Mom pronounced jokingly.

Sunday came, and I was genuinely excited about the possibility of Jerome and Giselle coming to church, but I was extremely tired too. I had talked to the kids late into Saturday night about all my adventures. Ruston believed that he was my protector and listened very intently to my story about the vandalism. I also explained to the kids the unbelievable blessing and joy of leading Giselle to the Lord. Becca and Ruston were excited about my courage to share my verse.

"You did it, Mom! Just like you said you would!" Becca exclaimed.

"God did it! I was just the vessel. I am so thankful He entrusted me with the opportunity."

I rehung the dishtowel that had fallen from the oven handle then abruptly snatched it back to remove it. Recalling the time I had caught a similar dishtowel on fire—clutz! I had learned through the school of clumsiness that dishtowels, pizza boxes, and plastic wrap needed to stay *away* from the oven and burners. Pressing my hands over my eyes and rubbing the last bit of tiredness from them, I contemplated my sleepless night. The night had stretched to morning, and I had been too keyed up to fall asleep last night, pent up with the thoughts of the break-in and vandalism done to my Jeep. Who would so viciously slash my tires, get in my car, but not steal anything?

I was going to waltz right into the closest ranger station by Monday morning after dropping the kids at school and get to the bottom of this. I'm not sure, but I also might need to thank the ranger for his help and see if there were any leads on the case. No, I did not want to see *him*. He is the one who gave me a ticket. I only wanted to ease my mind. Maybe some new evidence had turned up.

As I was imagining my calm yet persistent aura I would be demonstrating, my cell phone rang.

"Miranda, I know you were scheduled to come in at ten tomorrow, but Katy called me about a doctor's appointment. Can you adjust your day tomorrow?" Carrie asked politely.

"Of course, I'll be in early, just as soon as I drop the kids off at school."

"Thanks, Miranda. I'll have some cinnamon rolls coming out by then, ready for your professional taste-testing opinion," Carrie said, smoothing over the inconvenience of the schedule change.

Chapter 4

I brewed coffee, for the simple comfort of it, then went upstairs, sipping my steamy café au lait. At my bathroom vanity, I concentrated in the mirror, applying my makeup. Then I proceeded to flatten my hair with a straightener until if fell into glossy sections.

Becca ran into my bathroom with some yellow hair ribbons.

"Mom, can you fix my hair?" Becca begged.

"Absolutely, my lovely princess!" I said, smiling into the mirror in response.

I divided the top half of her hair and braided both sides. Then twisting them up in matching buns, I secured each braided bun with some bobby pins. Tying the ribbons in bows around the buns, they streamed down on either side of her head. Becca thanked me as I tied her dress in the back. Her teal corduroy dress and purple leggings matched her fun personality.

"Now, what am I going to wear?" I asked Becca as I gazed into my small closet. "Closets were never a priority forty years ago," shoving aside a few outfits on hangers.

Becca pulled out my favorite tall black boots from the bottom of my closet. Reaching back in she said, "Wear this," as she laid my skinny jeans, trendy turquoise shirt, and short darted brown corduroy jacket on the four-poster oak bed. "We can look like twins!" she proclaimed.

I layered some chunky yellow and turquoise bracelets on each of my wrists to tie our twin theme together. "I think we are hip and in style!" I said, surveying our put-together looks. We walked downstairs, and I saw that Ruston had gelled his hair and looked very handsome and grown-up. I pictured him as a man waiting for life to begin. He had finished getting ready an *hour* ago and his thumbs hammered on the controller, which was wirelessly connected to the game console and linked to the flat-screen TV.

"You are growing up too fast!" I said, wiping a tear from my long lashes. He got up and hugged me.

"Growing up is what kids do," Ruston said with a mature tone.

Becca jumped into our hug. It was a sweet moment. We drove to church and walked inside of God's Mountain View Church.

"Oh look! There they are!" I waved to Giselle and Jerome as they walked in the front foyer of the church. "You made it!" I said excitedly. Giselle and I hugged. Rock, who also attended our church, walked over and shook Jerome's hand.

"Good to be here," Jerome said. Giselle smiled in agreement. We got some iced coffee in the foyer and visited for a few minutes, regaling yesterday's ups and downs. As we walked into the sanctuary, I saw the park ranger who gave me the ticket near the front row. I don't think he saw me, though.

Oh wait, he just smiled a little in our direction.

We sat down near the back of the sanctuary. The worship was full of life and many people in the congregation lifted their hands. One singer led us in a song, which focused on the majesty of God. Even the grandest mountains paled in comparison to our most Holy God's power and beauty. Giselle and I smiled at the words. They rang true to both of us. I could see Jerome was touched during the sermon. He kept squeezing Giselle's hand when the pastor spoke the Word.

Pastor Rob's sermon was on Jonah:

We can all run...but we must run to God and His will. Running away will only take us longer to get to His purposes for our lives. Jonah 1:1–3 states,

> The word of the LORD came to Jonah son of Amittai: 'Go to the great city of Nineveh and preach against it, because its wickedness has come up before me.' But Jonah ran

away from the LORD and headed for Tarshish. He went down to Joppa, where he found a ship bound for that port.

After Jonah was eventually swallowed by a whale, he cried out to God.

> To the roots of the mountains I sank down; the earth beneath barred me in forever. But you, LORD my God, brought my life up from the pit. "When my life was ebbing away, I remembered you, LORD, and my prayer rose to you, to your holy temple."

Did you hear those verses found in Jonah 2:6–7? Jonah remembered God when his life ebbed away. Once Jonah was ejected out of the whale's mouth, onto dry land, he heard from God again. As stated in Jonah 3:1–2,

> "Then the word of the LORD came to Jonah a second time: "Go to the great city of Nineveh and proclaim to it the message I give you."

In verse 3, Jonah obeyed the word of the LORD and went to Nineveh. We read further from the text found in Jonah 3:8–10,

> The king and all the people responded: "But let people and animals be covered with sackcloth. Let everyone call urgently on God. Let them give up their evil ways and their violence. Who knows? God may yet relent and with compassion turn from his fierce anger so that we will not perish." When God saw what they did and how they turned from their evil ways, he relented and did not bring on them the destruction he had threatened.

Pastor Rob continued:

Why do we have to get to the point sometimes that Jonah did—to do the will of the Father? Running away from God is going to get you no satisfaction. You will be left empty, in a pit. However, notice that God spoke to Jonah a second time. He speaks to us today, too, and does not give up on us. Why God loves us even in our stubbornness, refusing to do His will. The very life He has called us to live.

In some ways, we should have a response like the Ninevites. They heard from God and His Word, humbled themselves, and obeyed. The Ninevites recognized the power of God. Whether you are the Christian that has turned away from God, like Jonah. Or you are like the Ninevites; you don't know God, you have been living in habitual sin, but maybe you want to know God. Maybe you have heard His Word today and want to put your life in Him. Right now, won't you come?"

The music rose from the praise team in a beautiful melody about needing the Savior. I saw Jerome and Giselle stand up and walk forward to the pastor. Ruston, Becca, and I looked at each other grinning and said a quiet "Yay!"

The pastor spoke these words as an encouragement and benediction: There is hope for those that choose to follow Him—eternal hope, which comes from accepting Jesus as our Lord and Savior.

He smiled over at Giselle and Jerome and introduced them to the church. (Everybody applauded.) The pastor continued:

What the world offers as quick refills of satisfaction leaves us empty. We receive treasures in heaven when we are committed to do His will. Matthew 6:21 states, "For where your treasure is, there your heart will be also." The filling and renewing of our hearts comes from the Holy Spirit. "But be filled with the Holy Spirit," found in Ephesians 5:18, clearly demonstrates what needs to *fill* our lives. The Holy Spirit enters our lives upon Salvation. He yields His power over our thought life, comforts us, and reveals Scriptural truths and guidance. Let us walk in the Spirit and go out to tell others about Him! Amen.

We invited Giselle and Jerome to my parent's house for lunch. I had caught Mom earlier and knew they had plenty of food to share. Giselle and Jerome were glowing with a joy and peace.

Giselle and Jerome had both given their hearts to the Lord and couldn't believe how much love they felt from God. My mom and dad seemed to really connect with the couple and spoke about possibly discipling them. They both readily agreed. Jerome, an athlete himself, was impressed with Dad's "glory days" of running track. Giselle enjoyed Mom's cooking and asked if they could practice together sometime. Giselle whispered shyly to me that Jerome had talked about marriage, and she would probably need help feeding that *man!*

Monday morning came with a few flurries.

"Hooray!" Becca jumped up and down, "It's snowing!"

Ruston and I looked at each other and the thoughts of shoveling snow and icy roads hit my mind. Ruston, unfortunately as the man of the house, had to help out a lot with the driveway and sidewalk maintenance.

"Well, it's a little early for the snow to stick. No shoveling yet. Be sure to dress warm."

After a quick breakfast of buttered grits, giving into my Southern-craving comfort food, we jumped in the Jeep.

"Hey, y'all…you guys…uh…sorry…do you have everything?" Sometimes being transplanted from Louisiana to Colorado left me tangled.

"Yes!" they replied.

I had moved to Colorado after I married Ethan. He had been transferred here. Colorado was an incredible gift to America. Though there had been some adjustments made in my life, I was so glad to live here. Carrie and Scott had also moved out here when they had seen job possibilities. I had talked to Carrie almost every day before they moved here, painting the town as one beautiful mecca in need of a coffee shop oasis. Scott's busi-

ness and accounting background, rounded with Carrie's entre-
preneurial spirit, worked well for their dream to become a reality.

When I got to work, Carrie was there.

"Hey there, Carrie!" I said as we hugged.

We had seen each other briefly at church, but we hadn't had a
chance to talk.

"I missed you and adult conversation! I am so glad to be back!"
Carrie announced emphatically.

"I am glad Casey and Stacey are feeling better," I said warmly.

"The twins are so happy to be back with their preschool
friends. They didn't even cry when I dropped them off earlier this
morning. They just ran to play with all their friends and toys!"

"Good morning, Carrie and Miranda!" Katy, the other barista,
said as she tied on her apron, wrapping it around her small waist
and joined us up front. Her miniature frame was built like an
athletic teen, even though she was twenty-two.

"Hi, Katy, I thought you had a doctor's appointment?" I
said curiously.

"I did. They got me through quicker than I expected."

"Who do you see? The clinic I go to always takes at least
two hours."

"It's the new doctor's clinic on River Street, called *In the Bag*."

"In the Bag?"

"Yeah, I didn't get it at first either. The receptionist said the
doc has this classic black bag that contains all his medical supplies. So getting well is *in the bag*!"

"Catchy! Katy, I hate to tell you this, but your shirt is inside out."

"Oh, silly me. I got dressed in the dark. I'll go change it around
in a minute."

"What do you mean *in the dark?* You didn't have any electricity?" I said jokingly.

"Well, sort of…yes. I forgot to pay my electric bill for the past
few months. I have to go by the office later and pay pronto."

"Katy, I'm so sorry. Do you need some money to pay it?"

"Thanks, but I have enough. I set up an online bill pay but got confused about the autopay setting. I'll get it sorted out," Katy said as she shrugged her shoulders. Her brilliant blonde hair swung forward as she turned and took a customer's order.

Her nonchalance made me feel nervous sometimes. I would be freaking out if my electricity had been turned off. I guess when you don't have kids, you can fly by the seat of your pants. Poor Katy, just last week she forgot what some customers had ordered and made me go ask them again. She said they scared her with their "smartness." It's weird, but Katy was smart too, just young and a little clueless. I recalled the conversation I had with her last week after she felt so intimidated by the customers.

"Katy, sometimes, when you think people have you all figured out, you tend to meet those expectations. If they think you're blonde and silly with no brain, then you might act like that. If you look them in the eye and speak confidently, they could potentially behave differently. Our human nature naturally pleases people, even when it goes in the wrong direction. Sometimes we just feel insecure and the more mistakes we make in front of people, the more inadequate we feel. Until we stop pretending like we don't know any better and give up all together. Once we stop striving to grow and mature, we neglect 'the gift within us.' Second Timothy 1:6–7 reminds us that, 'For this reason I remind you to fan into flame the gift of God, which is in you through the laying on of my hands. For the Spirit God gave us does not make us timid, but gives us power, love and self-discipline.'"

Katy had hugged me and thanked me for the encouragement.

I looked at Katy at this present moment and wondered if she remembered what we had talked about last week.

Katy turned and said, "You know, Miranda, I really need to be more proactive about my life and focus on the gifts God has given me."

"That's wonderful, Katy. What focus do you think God has directed you toward?"

"Working with senior adults. I believe God is showing me that I can make a difference with them. I'm already taking courses in college. Maybe I should consider nursing, like an LPN or RN degree and work in home health or something like that."

"Katy, you would be amazing as a nurse. I encourage you to pursue that degree field. You are very smart and can learn anything you put your mind to."

"I believe I will talk to my academic advisor tomorrow and see what can be done to restructure my courses." Katy's face looked radiant as she imagined a nursing career.

"God is guiding you. Keep trusting in Him."

"I will and...thanks."

I brewed the special blend of the day, Java Java Jane, and filled some orders of a frozen coffee, a cappuccino and a latte. I felt the joy of the Lord strengthen the work of my hands. The customers probably thought I was a bit loony that I seemed so happy. However I knew ministry was taking place, and I actually felt like I was a vessel used for Him and His purposes.

"Hey, Carrie, we are getting low on the mocha syrup. Can you grab me some?" I said, shaking the last of the chocolate liquid from the squeeze bottle.

"Sure, coming right up," Carrie called from the back. She appeared in a moment, with two bottles of the deliciously sweet chocolate syrup that we drizzle on top of the whipped cream. "Here you go."

"Thanks so much!"

"No problem. That was an easy request. Oh, by the way, Scott wanted me to ask you about some guy's *thumb-drive* that you found? Apparently, they came in Saturday looking for it."

"Oh my goodness! I completely forgot about that!" I said, looking dumbfounded. "Now where did I put that? I know, I put it in my apron pocket for safekeeping. Uh, which I later threw in the dirty clothes bin in the back. Let me go see," I said, walking swiftly.

Carrie hurried to follow me. "You mean the bin that I threw in the wash this morning?" Carrie's brows wrinkled in worry.

I reached inside the washing machine and inspected the soaked pockets of each of the aprons.

"Here it is!" I said triumphantly as I felt a hard rectangle piece of plastic in my hand. "Okay, I wouldn't normally do this. But I need to see if it works," I said, walking over to the office laptop, wiping the USB port on my brown apron, and then blowing on the tip with my breath. "Whooo." Plugging the metal tip into the USB port, I listened to the whirring of the computer begin to read the drive.

Carrie leaned over my shoulder, "Lord, I pray this works!" she said as I concentrated.

I double-clicked on the file as it popped up on my screen. "It's working!" I said. Suddenly, my eyes widened to the incredibly detailed images of…what?

"It looks like the interior workings of a motherboard or circuit plate," Carrie said.

"Wiring, setting switches, plastics, cellphones, CPU, and mother board components," I said as I read the notes. What is this? "What is this used for?" I wondered. The page on the computer screen was also covered with mathematical formulas, calculations, and trajectory diagrams.

"It can't be!" I looked shocked as I struggled to translate the Arabic words written at the bottom of the page. "The energy of this magnitude could destroy an entire city block…" the words said in Arabic. I spoke the cold words: "It's a bomb, Carrie. This is instructions for making a bomb." I felt my knees weaken and my arms go limp.

"Miranda. Are you okay?"

"No, I'm not okay. This could be a terrorist weapon like 9/11 all over again—or the commuter train in Spain when 191 people were killed with bombs from backpacks—or the Boston

Marathon bombers. Carrie, this is a bomb. I've watched the news. Unfortunately, I've heard what terrorists use. *I read what it said*," I said, punctuating each word.

Chapter 5

"What do you mean, *you read what it said?*" Carrie's eyes squinted. "I didn't see any English words. All I see is some squiggles and dots on this scanned document below the numbers," Carrie demanded.

"No right here, written in Arabic: 'the energy of this magnitude, could destroy an entire city block or government building,'" I haltingly translated.

"You speak…Arabic," Carrie inquired incredulously. "I didn't see that on your application under *other languages spoken.*"

"Well, I didn't think it would ever come in handy," I replied humbly. "Years ago, my aunt and uncle went to Yemen with a humanitarian medical relief group. They both had medical backgrounds and worked with area hospitals. I learned a little of the Arabic language when I stayed there with them, when I was twenty. I loved the people, especially the children. However, there is so much oppression over there. The call to prayer, to pray to Allah, screeched out day and night. It was absolutely eerie."

Carrie looked at me and said, "This is unbelievable. I can't believe we are standing in my office, while Katy is whipping up lattes for some of our customers, and we are discussing a possible terrorist attack. This shouldn't be happening in *our* town. We need to call the sheriff," Carrie said with a scared sound in her voice.

"We probably should call homeland security. I mean, this is big," I said grimly. "This is not your average bad kids' breaking and entering scheme…Carrie-*breaking and entering.* You don't think, that this…that this was…I…I'm in danger!"

"Miranda, what are you talking about?" Carrie asked with a white face.

"My Jeep, I am driving on the spare right now, I have gashes in the canvas top, and my stuff was all rifled through on Saturday when I was hiking. Those guys must have broken into my Jeep looking for the *thumb drive*," I said as I snapped my fingers.

Carrie looked at me with comprehension, "Scott talked with them—"

"Scott must have told them I was keeping it safe for them. He didn't know. He couldn't have known, that...oh no, I think they just pulled in to the parking lot. I've got to get out the back. I'm sorry, Carrie. You have got to cover me!" I said vehemently.

"Cover you?" she asked nervously.

"You know, make up something—like, 'I had to step out,' which of course I did—I do. I have got to go."

"God be with you," Carrie called to me.

Grabbing the thumb drive, I ran out the back door. As I ran outside, a sickening feeling caused my feet to grind to a halt.

"Oh, this is not fair!" I muttered. I can't drive away without my keys. I hurriedly thought through my options:

a. Sneak back in there and get my keys.

b. Run down the street with highly volatile information and get help.

c. There is no C.

Wait, I think I see a guy in uniform across the street, maybe he can help. Sprinting from the back parking lot of Bean Me Up, I prayed I would make it without being seen. Regardless of the cars on the busy street, I broke a world record (well, probably just a personal record...but I was fast). I raced across four lanes of traffic to the other side. Panting, I reached for the shoulder of the officer as he turned to look at me.

"Oh no, Mr. Park Ranger?" I said audibly.

"What did you call me?"

"Uh, sorry, no…um…great! Yea! Maybe you can help me? No really, *you have to help me!*" I said desperately.

I think he could tell that I was in some sort of trouble as I looked over my shoulder again.

"Okay, what's wrong?" he asked. I just plunged right in detailing the documents and images that I had seen, sharing about the Arabic quote at the bottom of the page. I spilled out my story in broken sentences while waving the USB drive in the air.

"And you say that they are here, right now, in the coffee shop?"

Just then the two Yemenis guys came out of Bean Me Up and began pointing across the street—*at me!*

"Get in," he said, pointing to his Range Rover.

I jumped into the passenger seat with a yelp, climbing over his duffel bag and jamming myself into the small space beside the center console. He slammed into gear and took off and, within minutes, left the town and valley behind.

The park ranger got on his cell phone and spoke tersely. At the time I vaguely wondered why he didn't get on his radio and call for backup. He was driving and talking into his phone so fast, I was wondering what he was even saying.

Something about "We've found them. Yeah, I have the files. They are giving us chase. *Operation Bait and Trap* has been activated."

I looked back and saw their black truck behind us. I don't know why, but in that moment, I leaned back in my seat, tightened my seat belt, and closed my eyes. Maybe it was just the shock of everything.

"Hang on," he said as he nosed the accelerator down to the floor.

Apparently, his Range Rover had some kick. I felt my back ease into the seats, like they were molded in, my feet bolted down. The rate of our speed, combined with a mountain hairpin turn, made me lose my precarious position, and I leaned hard into the leather covered console.

"You okay?" he asked.

"Yes, I'm fine," I said.

My eyes were open now—wide. His hands gripped the steering wheel. His chiseled jaw clenched slightly as we roared along. *Strong.* He looked strong. I knew that he could take care of me at that moment, and I completely trusted him. I know, I know, I had little choice, but it felt heaven-sent. I began to pray for our safety and for wisdom as he drove. I felt the Holy Spirit speaking over *me* with a peace, and I knew that a balm was placed on my heart.

"Next straight away, can you hand me something out of my duffel bag?" he asked. As we bounced along the back road, I shifted my weight slightly to have a better look in his gear bag. Unzipping it, my eyes locked into the items inside: a few guns, bullets, magazine casings, some electronic devices, some climbing gear and some MREs. I thought about my own duffel bag in comparison. *What in the world is all this...and I thought I was prepared?*

"Hand me my M-4 assault rifle," he said, pointing to the gun that was the longer than the length of a man's arm. "Be careful, it's loaded, but the safety is on."

"Here," I said, gingerly as I handed it to him.

Without warning, a ping hit the back windshield.

"Get down," he said. "They just made us a target."

I tried not to freak out while I assumed crash position. The park ranger slammed on his breaks, threw the SUV into park, and got out, hastily getting off an abundance of shots with his assault rifle. The terrorist shot back, bullets ricocheted off our vehicle like hail on a tin roof. I had never been shot at, and the whole experience was deafening to my ears. To say it lightly, I was unnerved. Honestly, I was terrified. I felt tense and sick with fear. After another quick burst from the guys behind us, the park ranger peeled out. We drove further up the steep mountain road, feeling twisted and bent like a spoon left in a disposal.

"I'm gonna need you to help me for a sec."

I nodded weakly.

"Here, hold the wheel."

I grabbed the wheel, leaning to my left, while he unclipped his M-9 semiautomatic handgun from his waist. He clicked off the safety and released another fifteen rounds, emptying the magazine clip on the truck behind us. Their truck rocked back as the driver's slowed and kept a distance.

"Do you still have that thumb drive?" he asked, calmly taking the wheel again.

"Yes, here it is," sliding it out of my pocket.

"Plug it into the computer. We can download the information," he directed as he indicated the laptop mounted to the dashboard.

I worked quietly for a while getting the images downloaded. Occasionally, the park ranger glanced over and murmured to himself about terrorists making a mess of this town.

"It's finished," I said.

"Okay, now we are going to send it," he said.

"You probably realize there is no satellite signal range out here," I said, a little bit confused, noting the surrounding mountains.

"True for a normal day in the mountains," he said, smiling, revealing an amazing smile.

"But today is no ordinary day. And I am no *ordinary* park ranger. Can you hand me another box magazine? No, not those, the shorter ones. Good, that's the ones I want. Here, hold the wheel, again." He reloaded his M-9 pistol, hearing a registered click as the magazine slid into place then leaned out the window, and with careful calculation shot at the truck behind us. He then reholstered his gun and continued the relaxed conversation, like he had just waved to a neighbor.

I gladly handed the wheel back and nodded, wide-eyed.

"In that bag of tricks over there"—glancing at the duffel bag—"contains a cell booster and satellite phone. The computer will sync with the cell phone and then we can transmit the info from the thumb drive. Its government grade and has enough juice to amp out a message to the Russian Space Station if we wanted to! I want you to e-mail this to roberthelding@jttf.gov. He's my boss and can get this to the right people."

He breathed out and said passionately, "We are gonna protect the city, no matter the cost. I actually work with a Domestic Joint Terrorism Task Force. I've been stationed down here for a few months after we monitored some chatter in this area. I am a Ranger, but not really a park ranger. I'm a major in the United States 75th Army Ranger Regiment. The park ranger gig was my cover, but it also kept me occupied enough to gain access to the sleeper units in the area. I worked the grid from here to Salix, supervising the personnel who track the online users and integrating the main eavesdropping program the NSA has developed. We've been sweeping calls, noting the duration of the calls, checking the caller and receiver names, and matching them to a terrorist organization."

"Does that mean you've been listening to every call made in town…like when my mom taught me how to cook chicken?"

The major chuckled. "No, I didn't hear that one. Actually we listen to very few conversations. It's mostly hard data that we are assessing. If we do find a match to a name that may be red-flagged in the system, we have to go to a federal judge to listen to the conversations. However, when it comes to a potential terrorist attack, the government is going to give us a green light. Which they did. I followed protocol on all areas. I was getting close to linking the smaller based units here in Mountain View to Salix, where a larger sleeper group had formed.

"Wait, are you telling me that there are terrorists that have been living in this town?"

"Potentially, these guys could have been here for years. That's their MO. They lay low, don't draw attention to themselves, and then unleash a fireball of an attack without warning. It's a dangerous game, and it makes finding these guys so challenging."

"But you said you found them?"

"Yeah, they slipped up. Chatter has increased. Our decoding equipment has been analyzing data 24-7 and began to make the links about a week ago. I've been trying to gather resources and formulate a plan for arresting these guys along with the larger organization and connections," he said as the Range Rover gripped the road in a swift turn.

"It's challenging, isn't it? Some people would maintain that 'monitoring' could limit freedom of speech," I asked as I elbowed the shifting bag next to me and resettled in my seat.

"We want it *all* here in America, freedom to live and the ability to maintain that freedom."

"We do, but some people need to remember that freedom has a cost. Freedom has to be protected and isn't natural to mankind," I added.

"You understand what is at stake every day. I consider it my duty and privilege to preserve that freedom," he proclaimed with rigid determination edging his voice.

"As I think about what is currently at issue, according to the thumb drive I found, the terrorists had plans for a bomb. So when and where is the bomb they are building supposed to be detonated?"

"We don't have all those details in yet. Based on our current intel, we knew something big was happening and that it was soon. We believe that the bomb they had planned needed another shipment of explosive material. That obstacle was the delay that we needed to tie up the loose cords of the operation."

"Their mistake with the USB flash drive has driven them out of hiding. Does this mean the plans they had for Mountain View could be escalating to a current time frame?" My eyes were wide with question.

"Unfortunately, these terrorist come with a full arsenal of the enemy at their disposal. We are dealing with an interlinked group that has money and connections. If we don't stop them, the attack could take place very soon, indeed."

"Why here? What did our little town do to anybody?" I fretted, feeling vulnerable at the thought.

"I am aware of what this town means to you. It means something to me as well. Mountain View is the epitome of small-town America. That's why they want to make a statement here. America, at its core, is made up of small towns filled with good people. The terrorists see it differently. America to them is a rejection of radical Islamism. Therefore they reject all Westerners. The hate is strong and fed to these fundamental groups since childhood."

Under that cool and tough exterior was a man who loved America and her freedom. I thought of my kids at school and swallowed hard. I knew my parents were picking them up because it was supposed to be my late day at work. I prayed for them. At least one thing in my day was going to go right. Typing in the sender, hitting the attachment button, I clicked *send*.

"Bang! Bang! Bang, bang!" The back window was being hit multiple times with a semiautomatic. Our vehicle echoed with the bullets scraping the paint off the car and dinging the roof.

"I am surprised the windows haven't broken yet. Not that I want it to or anything," I quickly added as I crouched down further.

I heard him chuckle confidently. He smiled at me and said, "I have a few upgrades that your average park ranger is missing on his vehicle. Bullet-proof glass is one of them."

"These, uh, modifications, was something you did?" I asked with a questioning look.

"Well, I know a few people. A few connections with other agencies. We knew that things could get bad. I wanted to be prepared," he spoke, unfazed as the bullets continued to zip past the SUV.

The road was getting steeper with every turn.

"We should be reaching the pass soon," I said. I knew that the pass was usually snowed in, even at this time of year. We were going to be trapped if we continued driving in this direction much longer. "What's your plan?" I asked, trying to stay calm.

"Keep driving for as long as we can—help is on the way," he said assuredly.

"How do our rescuers know where we are?" I wondered aloud.

"I have a tracking beacon installed on the vehicle. It transmits GPS coordinates with every turn," he said as he reached over and touched my shoulder. "We are going to be okay. God is with us. I have been praying for us. God has a plan that is bigger than we could fathom. Let's let Him lead."

I looked back into his green eyes for just a moment. That brief encounter caught at my heart. I felt that sense of trust and connection. It was nice to meet someone who cared for me, and he really loved God. Wow, that's a nice package, I mused.

"Have you ever climbed before?" he questioned.

"Does climbing on an artificial rock wall on a cruise ship count?" I said, slightly embarrassed.

"Anything counts at this point." He accented his answer with a smile.

"Why do you ask?" I asked, trying to suppress the panicked lurch in my stomach.

"See that climbing gear in the bag? We may have to climb when the road ends and get a little higher than the terrorists. They know that we've seen them, and they don't know that we have already transmitted their plans. They are on a mission to kill!" he said in a growl.

The Range Rover came to a grinding halt as we reached the pass. The snowbanks toppled around our tires with a permanence I didn't want to predict. The major grabbed his M-4 again and picked off the terrorists' SUV in the distance. The bullets seemed to slow them down when suddenly we watched as their truck swerved off the road.

"I got one of their tires," he said, slightly gratified.

"Does that mean we're safe for the moment?" I asked with hope etching my voice.

"For the moment," the major said. "We are going to have to keep moving, though. These men won't let a flat tire stop them."

I saw the two guys flipping a spare onto the road. They began jacking up the back of the left side of the truck. Their movements seemed agitated and angry with one another.

"Things are not going according to their plans," he murmured with a glint of amusement.

"They have you to thank for that," I said, slightly relieved.

"I don't think I'll be getting any thanks from them. Probably all I'll be accepting is bullets aimed at us as tokens of their appreciation. Okay, it's time to go," he stated flatly.

I agreed with an acquiescence that surprised me. What was I not willing to do with this man? If he had said we were going to ride tigers with pink lanterns on our heads, I would have said—yes.

Grabbing our gear, the major filled an empty backpack with some provisions, a belay, pulley, a bag of rope, an ice axe, and some magazine cartridges for his M-9. He then helped steady me as I stepped into a harness. He swiftly attached a nylon rope through some loops on the front of my lanyard, stitched to the front of my harness. He opened and spun his carabiners to the various cams and attached them to his harness.

"If you stay flat against the rock and keep your knees spread slightly, you can get more of an anchor in your footholds. Make sure you achieve a secure toe hook, which is wedging your toes into the mountain, and remember to clench your fingers into a stronghold, closing your knuckles and thumbs together to crimp onto the rock," he instructed.

"I can do this with God's help," I said, breathing a prayer for strength.

We scuttled off to the left of the base of the snow-covered mountain and shoed our way up the bottom portion. It was slick and rocky. Crusty snow and sheets of ice coated the vertical soil and rocks. He freehanded ahead of me slightly. I could see his veins in his neck bulge as he fought against the mountainside.

The snowy rocks coated in an icy film made me feel precarious. I tried not to think about slipping as I cautiously maneuvered up the mountain's face. As the mountain slope sharply bent up, the major grabbed a cam-lanyard duo and wedged it tightly into the rock above him. He then stretched his foot to gain a firm outcropping. From here on out, we were going to need equipment to survive. Off in the distance, we saw the truck move back onto the road.

"This is it, game on again," he said decisively.

We strengthened our resolve and climbed upward. I could feel my hamstrings beginning to waver as I exerted more energy pressing skyward toward the top. Far below, we heard the crunch of tires and the squeal of the breaks as they came to a rest and the rapid talk of discussion. They were looking at the SUV. As I glanced down, I saw one of them take a butt of a rifle and attempt to knock out the windows while the other one held a black metal object. "I think one guy is trying to break into your car with a crowbar," I whispered as my heart sank.

"That's a waste, but we have what we need," he said, adjusting his backpack. We continued to gain altitude on the rock's surface. I could see that the scope of the landscape below was becoming smaller.

"Do you think they will follow us?"

"They probably don't have any climbing gear. We need to put some distance between us and get above that ledge before they figure out where we are. Once they locate us they *will* shoot at us."

I knew it wouldn't be long before they found our footprints and followed us up the slope. Whether they could climb or not wasn't a question in my mind. They had guns. We were now easier targets because we couldn't dodge bullets being pinned down on the mountain's face.

"What kind of people would shoot at defenseless climbers?" I wondered aloud.

"Unfortunately, I know these guys," he said in contempt.

"I have been studying their movements for a month now. They were trained in a Taliban training camp. They have prepared their life to be jihadist. At any moment, they are willing to give up their life for their cause. They believe it will bring them greater happiness in the afterlife."

"Ppffff," I snorted. "They're in for a real surprise when they get to death's doorway," I said as we scaled higher.

"Yes, but they don't know that. The extreme teaching they've been brainwashed into believing has created a generation of men who have no qualms about taking lives. They are not going to quit until they have taken ours."

Chapter 6

Adrenaline took over at this point, and we both seamlessly climbed. Stretching, reaching for the next crevice and hand-hold, pushing up, and moving upward. I followed right below the major. He clamored forward, reaching beyond human bounds. We were connected by a red and blue nylon webbing rope that had a tubular shape.

"Are you in a good spot for the moment? Can you hold on?" he asked from further up the rock face.

"Yeah, I've got a little ledge right here."

"Good. Now untie the rope."

I unclicked the carabiner and yanked the rope in approval. The rope grew slack and whipped up the mountain to where he was.

"I'm changing the length," he said as he inserted the cam into the crevice and attached it to the end of the stem through a sling and carabiner. "Here, grab my rope and loop it through. He had attached the pulley on his end and planned to pull me up."

"I can barely...reach...it." The doubled rope he had lowered was just beyond my grasp.

"Torque it!" he said fervently.

I gave a small leap and reached for it just as snow melted under my shoe. The snow movement caused rocks to shatter down, pin-pointing our exact location to the men below.

"They've spotted us! They are starting to climb up!"

Clumsily, due to nerves and the cold, I tried unsuccessfully to clip the carabiner to my harness. I tried again, and this time I heard a satisfying snap as the carabiner clicked in place.

"Ready," I said as he began to pull me up the sheer cliff. I couldn't help but look down at the dizzying height below. Gunfire kicked up snow and rocks around my feet and head.

"Hurry, pull!" I said windily, kicking the air.

"I've got you," he called. With a final, mighty lunge from the major, I felt myself yanked up onto a shelf of rock. I rested my back and breathed for the first time—in what felt like...an hour. A smattering of gunfire continued to loosen rocks below, shuttling down snow all the way to the bottom.

"How high are we now? Are we almost to the top?"

The major checked his altimeter located on the face of his digital watch. "It's measuring 150 feet vertical rise from the ground. Once we get through the rest of this sheer face, I'd say we should be close."

The extent of my view, as I peeked over the tips of my shoes, was dizzying. The way down was long, and the way up looked arduous, if not impossible. I think anyone would be afraid of heights due to the icy, slick rocks and the sheer expanse of the mountain before me. I felt the fear of my situation, clamp down on me. I was afraid of falling. The terrorists with their guns terrified me. I needed to survive for my kids' sake. They already lost a "normal family." A "normal mom" was the best I could do. My heart took a determined beat. I planned on surviving, but I knew I wouldn't make it out of here without assistance, or let's face it, a miracle.

"When is that 'help' supposed to arrive?" I asked with a disconcerted look.

"It's not going to be long. I didn't tell you this before, but climbing up here was really a trap for the terrorists. We are the bait. *Operation Bait and Trap* was going to involve me and a few experienced Army Rangers setting a trap for the terrorists. We had planned on 'locating' the missing package they needed for their bomb then lead them to believe that some rebellious, disenfranchised, renegades wanted in on the action. You finding the thumb drive and the terrorist attempting to recover it sped up the plan for today."

"Oh," is all I could manage for a reply.

"I'm sorry it had to involve you, but that's life." He looked at me with regret filling his eyes. "Right now, we've got the terrorists locked in on a steep mountainside with nowhere to turn. They might be working their way up toward us, but what they don't know is what is coming at them from behind. We need to bide our time and trust the plan that is in motion. Look, you're doing great. Even a seasoned climber would have been challenged by this climb. You are really pushing through. I am proud of you."

His words made my heart soar like a bird, being released from captivity.

I smiled and said, "Oh, it wasn't that hard. Especially, when I got an elevator ride."

"Hey, you climbed most of it. You're a natural!" he said warmly. His eyes clicked with mine, and for a moment, I wanted to imagine that this was an exciting date.

"I never asked you, what's your name?"

"My name is Michael. Michael Taylor," he said charmingly.

Just then, the sound of whirring helicopter blades slashed through my momentary date-on-a-ledge experience.

"The cavalry is here."

On the ground, guys dressed out in black and gray camo took well-aimed shots at the tires of the terrorists' truck. Their vehicle sunk down instantly.

"They're not going anywhere," Michael announced emphatically as he pulled a miniature binocular set out from his jacket and zeroed in on the action below. "Ground troops have appeared and are taking a few shots at the guys. The two terrorists are trapped—okay, one of them just slid down to the base of the mountain. He's surrounded. Now—if I can get a shot off, anything after fifty meters is a going to be a prayer with this gun," but Michael aimed his gun and the bullet hit the remaining terrorist near his shoulder. The ice he was clinging to broke off and he fell backward. "That might sting a little."

I watched as the guy grappled for some icy rocks then fell to the earth, at least fifteen feet below.

"It's a complete takedown!" Michael said exuberantly.

"That's amazing, and I am happy that the operation went so well, but there is one problem—we're still stuck here," I said, shivering slightly.

Michael looked at me and held out his hand. "Ready to finish this mountain?"

I nodded with enthusiasm.

"Okay, let's tallyho!" Michael stood and reached forward onto the next handhold; when out of nowhere, two long lime-green nylon rope ends were thrown down and swayed in front of our faces.

"You guys need a hand down there?" a voice called.

I squeaked out a "Yes!"

Michael helped secure both our ropes, gave them a tug, and shouted, "Belay on." I felt my body lift up the mountain. My feet dangled freely, for a moment, then I was swung into the side of the mountain. Gripping the snow and rocks, I pushed away. I moved upward swiftly until I felt two arms pull me up to the top. I was staggered by the sight of a group of United States Army Ranger soldiers.

"Thank you. Thank you!" I said to the soldiers, still stunned by the turn of events. Michael was getting his back hit in congratulatory pounds; his arm was practically shook off as he was acknowledged by all his buddies at the top.

"Sir," a young lieutenant walked sharply over. "Good news, the terrorists are in custody. The reports and chatter are being monitored. We are hunting up any sleeper groups and cross analyzing all the new data you sent us via satellite."

"General Helding is on the phone for you," a sergeant said, handing him a cell phone.

Michael smiled and held a look of gratitude as he listened to the man on the phone. "Thank you, sir. You too. Okay. Good-bye."

On top of that beautiful mountain, Michael walked over to me and hugged me for a long time.

"I guess I can finally start calling you Michael instead of Mr. Park Ranger," I said shyly. Michael laughed. "Maybe I can get you a ride off this mountain," he said softly. "In exchange for a date? Unofficially of course."

"A ride home—then, yes, maybe I can work it into my busy schedule. Just...don't ask me to cook for you!"

Michael laughed harder this time. "Can't cook, can't drive slowly, uh-oh, I'm in trouble."

"I *can* make a mean cup of coffee!" I said, spouting off slightly.

"You know I was going to come into Bean Me Up today to see you, when you found me!" Michael told me fondly.

"*Today?* Today was a million hours and miles ago." I spoke from somewhere else. The day was truly catching up with me.

"And miles to go until I sleep," Michael quoted from Frost sounding slightly fatigued. "Look. I am going to be busy with the aftershocks of debriefing for a while. One of *these guys* will be happy to take you where you need to go," Michael had said the last words loud enough for the group to hear.

Two soldiers promptly stepped forward and offered to drive me down in their Humvee. There was an old logging road ahead that lead back to a main highway.

"Where to, ma'am?"

"To 137 Larkspur Lane—it's near Jade Avenue," I told the young men, reciting my address sleepily before engaging with a much-needed rest.

Even if I was bounced around a bit in the back seat, I was safe. I felt my body, weighed down with the heaviness of sleep, each muscle relaxing as I eased down into a blissful slumber. I heard the Humvee and voices before I opened my eyes.

"Ma'am, you're home," one soldier said.

My parents and children ran to meet me on the front steps of the house in an elated group hug. "What a story!"

"We're so glad you're safe!"

"I can't believe…we had no idea, until Major Taylor called us."

Everyone was talking and laughing. It was beautiful standing there surrounded by my people. My safe and free family! The Humvee rolled back down the driveway, releasing a surreal feeling over me.

"I think I was at war today," I said, trying to blink the tears from my eyes.

My dad pulled me into a hug and told me, "Sugar, it's going to be all right. You're safe, we're safe."

Mom came and wrapped her arms around me. "Like he said, Miranda, honey, thank God you're okay."

I hugged her tight.

"Is it true you were fired upon by an AK-47?" Ruston asked with a respect in his tone.

I gave him a long hug. We walked inside the house, and Mom got me some blankets.

"I was so cold up there," I said, shivering slightly.

Becca snuggled close to me. Dad quickly built a fire in the fireplace that could have outdone any pyromaniac. I shared as best I could the details that led up to today.

"You're telling me that you carried a terrorist plot in your apron pocket," Dad asked incredulously.

"I know, it sounds ridiculous, but I had no idea, until I looked at the files," I said, trying to sound less like a little girl that was threatening to rise up in me.

"What a survival story," Ruston said. "Mom, you climbed a mountain with your bare hands. You got shot at. You are a legend!"

I laughed weakly at his acclimations. "I had a lot of help surviving today." Closing my eyes, I could see Michael's hands reaching out to me on the side of the mountain.

"Dear, what was the man's name that called?" Mom asked Dad.

"Michael," I interrupted his answer. "Michael has become a good friend through all this. He is a strong Christian and really helped me keep me calm through this entire ordeal," I said as I leaned into the couch again, feeling a little dizzy.

"Well, we want to meet him," Mom said with a knowing smile.

Mom and Dad spent the night and planned to leave in the late morning after breakfast. I was glad to have their comforting presence as I drifted off to sleep that night in my own, comfortable bed.

Michael called two days later late one evening. I was already asleep, but I answered on the second ring.

"Miranda?" Michael asked tentatively.

"Hello, Michael," I said a little drowsily.

"We are just finishing up here. Got the down-low on much of the enemies' activities. I can't share it all with you, but you should know that we apprehended some more terrorist cells!" he said with excitement in his voice.

"Awesome! How are you doing?" I asked.

"I'm doing fine. How are you feeling?" he asked tentatively.

"Apart from being scraped up a little, I'm fine too," I said as I gently touched a bruise on my arm.

"God is good! I have thanked God that we made it out of there. It was a tough spot," Michael said.

"I praise God for you as well. It would be a different story had you not been there," I said.

"A story that I wouldn't want to know the ending to. I'm so glad you're not seriously hurt. I guess I better call it a night," he said with regret in his voice.

"Good night," I said quietly.

Chapter 7

The next day, an official car pulled up to the house.

Ruston called me from the kitchen, "Mom, somebody's here."

I wiped my hands on a towel and shook my hair, bunching a few curls together with my hands. I had showered today and had makeup on (which was a notch in any mom's belt).

"Who is it?" I said as I walked to the front door.

Two men stood in uniform. One of them was none other than *Michael*. Michael was dressed in full dress blues. I took in his army uniform with the golden oak leaf insignia of major, his military haircut shaded dark black, his long legs and strong build standing correctly. "May I introduce, General Robert Helding of the United States Army," Michael said proudly.

The general shook my hand, saying, "Ma'am, what an honor. We've had a lot of, shall we say, professionals, trying to uncover the details of this terrorists' plot. None of them could have done a better job than you. Thank you for your service to our country." The general smiled at me and the children. "Young man, young lady, both of you can be very proud of your mom," General Helding said, putting his hands on Ruston and Becca's shoulders.

"Oh we are, sir," Ruston said with an enthusiastic smile. Becca nodded, smiling too.

The coffee shop bustled with the clanking of spoons, chuckles from gathered friends, and the rattle of the newspaper. I was serving my twentieth customer before I had time to glance at the digital chrome clock—9:00 a.m. The secretive sun was peeking into the windows, warming the front of the shop. I breathed in, amazed that I was here working with such everyday occurrences, like people drinking coffee. Mountain View was safely restored to the small-town order it had always known. Some people who lived in the high country would not have heard about all the activity over the past week, if it hadn't been for the town paper, *Mountain View Sentinel*. A full front-page article had featured the details of the terrorist plot.

"And I quote, '*It was uncovered by our very own Miranda Colvin.*' Miranda, I think you have some explaining to do…" Carrie said.

"Yeah, give us some details," Katy said, leaning her arms onto the counter.

"As you both are aware, the USB drive was found right under that table," I said, pointing to the corner booth.

"Oooh, we should put a sign there telling people that they are sitting at the same table as the terrorists. Like the old hotels do with the famous bad boys of the Wild West," Katy said, imagining grandly.

"I'll think about it. Our business has doubled since the report went out. Scott's plans to add on may become not only ideal but necessary after all. Everybody wants to shake your hand, Miranda, and see where it all began," Carrie said, regripping her hands together in a nervous gesture.

"Look, I know that y'all were concerned for me. I'm sorry that you had to talk to them after I left. What did you say?"

"I tried to be calm. I couldn't talk much, and my legs were shaking like crazy. I told them you weren't here. Then they ran outside. I guess that's when they followed you?"

"They saw me from across the street and it's a blur after that. So you are okay?"

"I'm fine. The only item that the coffee shop lost was when some agents of the Terrorism Task Force came in yesterday and seized the computer we used to view the contents of the USB drive."

"Oh, Carrie, I'm sorry for the inconvenience," I said, apologizing again.

"Miranda, this is not your fault. The town is safe because of your…curiosity and fortitude. After all the adventures we've been through growing up, I'm not surprised at the circumstances that have unfolded."

"I'm glad you didn't get hurt. You probably saved my life. Had they caught me before I ran into Michael…I…" My voice shook, and I shuddered.

Carrie hugged me tight and said, "We weren't harmed."

"Carrie, did you tell all this to the authorities?"

"I did. They questioned everyone in the shop. It was stressful. Mostly because, from what I understand, the men who we dealt with had a bomb that was close to being completed."

"It's true. The chatter Michael had overheard was that the makings of the bomb was on an accelerated time clock. They were waiting on the last shipment of material."

"I can't believe we came so close to a terrorist attack," Katy said soberly.

"God intervened. I thank God for His hands of mercy," I said, moved by the emotional release of His love and grace on my life.

"Now, tell me again why you understand Arabic?" Carrie looked at me curiously, like I was an unknown bird she had discovered.

"I spent a summer in Yemen with my aunt and uncle. Carrie, you were in Europe that summer, so that's why you didn't remember. Before I went over there, I studied Arabic off and on for a year with a language program. My mom had bought an Arabic audio series and some workbooks. It was specifically designed for learning to speak the Arabic language for use in Yemen. I used to listen to it exclusively in the car every day when I commuted to downtown New Orleans from our house in old Metairie. I don't know why I enjoyed it so much, but I guess now it makes sense. When I read the Arabic report on the diagram, everything clarified, and I could recall the language like I had just been there. It's not surprising that God used my specific dialect of the Arabic language to understand the Yemenis terrorists. There are so many dialects of the Arabic language, it's a miracle that I could read it at all. God knew what He was doing ten years ago."

My attention was diverted as I assisted some customers with their orders of caramel macchiatos. I prepared them by layering steamed milk and froth, poured a shot of espresso through the middle, and then artistically drizzled sweet caramel across the top. The customers seemed delighted as they turned away taking indulgent sips. I was pleased at their satisfaction. This was a good outlet for me, working in a coffee shop as a barista. I never grew tired of the coffee scent that hung heavy in the air.

After the pace slowed down for a moment, Carrie asked me to continue sharing about my experience in Yemen.

"My aunt and I would go on home visits, careful to dress conservatively and covering our heads with a hijab. Once we had arrived in a home, we would dip our hands in a bowl of water for cleansing. We would always visit only women, as it wouldn't have been appropriate otherwise. The lovely women would be so serious on the streets, covered from head to toe, but once we entered their homes, the Yemenis women were warm and funny. Some of them even dressed quite modern under their outer garments.

"Really? Like jeans?"

"Yes, or a skirt and a shimmery blouse. It was really surprising. A burqa or niqab may inhibit their personalities. When they are in a safe setting, the women are completely different."

"That's amazing, I never would have imagined that."

"Oh, and how they liked to dance! We would eat popcorn and talk nonstop. My favorite culinary experience was the Bint Al Sahn, layered bread covered in honey. I also enjoyed drinking the strong black tea made with cardamom seeds, cloves, sugar, and milk that was served in the homes. The people of Yemen are very special, and I know that God provided that window to share His love to a people He created. I won't be able to return now due to the political unrest. My time there was sacred."

"It sounds like an amazing experience," Carrie said then turned to help a customer that had just walked up to the counter.

I looked over the coffee shop and noticed how the people that came through the doors were fascinating. Each table was filled with a story unfolding. A businessman with his laptop busily typed and reconfirmed figures. Three women seemed amused by something that was said, as laughter peeled out over the stained concrete floor. An elderly couple discussed the weather as they sat by the window. A husband readjusted his tartan beret as the wife leaned forward to change it back. A bearded professor pushed his glasses up his nose and then picked up a stack of term papers to grade. A tired woman held a book, taking a moment to escape in enjoyable peace. The people were a rainbow of lives, woven by God, each needing a touch from Him. I prayed for each customer that God would give them a good day filled with His love and purpose.

Just then, the door opened to the coffee shop, and the sharp heels of a very important person clipped across the tile floor... Mrs. Liddenaul. She was a "crucial" member of several boards for local organizations, and she also served as a civil "servant," organizing a census (about ten years ago) and promoting suitable and necessary laws to be passed in our community (or at least in her mind). Carrie dove into the back office, muttering about some documentation that was an absolute priority at the moment, leaving me readily available. Most people were easy to serve, but there were some that required patience.

"Good morning, Mrs. Liddenaul. What would you like to order?"

"Ms. Miranda…" She noted my name tag in a piercing glance, like it was our first meeting. "I would like a mocha cappuccino. Now, the coffee must be made exact. I would like equal—I mean equal parts of perfectly measured espresso with steamed milk, the cocoa must be introduced at the top with a dollop of fresh cream, and no canned whip—*ever*." Her stern demeanor indicated that I was her pupil under her careful tutelage.

Presenting her coffee to her, she eyed it suspiciously then nodded, paid, and left. I hoped to break through her outer shell and get to know this prickly individual.

Two weeks passed before Michael called me again. I had started to wonder if I would hear from him again.

"Can I officially ask you on a date this Saturday?" Michael asked with a hopeful sound in his voice.

I cleared my voice. "Two things. First, in my family, you are going to have to meet my dad before we go on any dates. I am not counting our date-on-a-ledge as date material."

Michael chuckled and said. "Okay, did that, what next?"

"You what?" I floundered.

"I met your parents with General Helding. The general said, 'A girl raised with that much passion for America, must have some great parents—let's go meet them.' Once a general has an idea in his head…well, you would have to have an entire army to try and stop him, which I don't recommend."

"They never told me," I said, feeling surprised and slightly stunned.

"Your dad wanted it to be a surprise when I called you," Michael said, enjoying himself.

"Oh, so that's why Mom and Dad seemed so happy this past week. Every time I mentioned that you hadn't called…um, never mind. So what were you saying…?" My voice trailed off.

"You said, two things. Meet your dad and what else? What other hoop can I jump through for you?" Michael asked.

"Oh *right*, the other 'thing.' The other 'thing' is that Bean Me Up needs their computer back. Can you take care of that?" I asked in a serious tone.

Michael started to laugh and laugh.

"Are you there?" I asked dolefully.

"Their computer will be returned this week. Now about that date?" Michael commanded lightly.

Snow covered the front yard as it had been steadily snowing all week long. I kept peeking out of my bedroom window hoping to catch a glimpse of my date. Michael should be here any minute. I had dressed in a black dress overlaid in Italian lace that hit above the knee. Its classic slim lines paired with my heeled boots felt lovely. I glanced at the mirror and saw the auburn highlights glowing in my curls. *Not bad for a mom of two*, I thought as I swiped my nose with powder and retouched my shimmery rouge lipstick one more time. Mom and Dad were outside building a snowman with the kids when Michael arrived promptly at 5:00 p.m. After the kids and my mom said hello, my dad and Michael shook hands. I loved watching my family interact with him. Michael began helping with the now, *ginormous* snowman. I could see Becca and Ruston, from my view, add more snow to the base and point out to Michael where the snowman needed more height. Michael obliged them by reaching up high and patting more snow on the head. I watched for just another minute then came downstairs.

"Michael!" I said with my heart beating as I stood on the front porch.

"Wow!" Michael said in a long breath.

Michael's deep green eyes were only for me as he walked up the front steps and hugged me for a moment.

My family talked to Michael for what felt like an hour. Finally, we got in his new granite-colored SUV and drove into town. I sat in my seat, smoothing my black dress, touching my silver necklace and experiencing myself as…beautiful. I wasn't feeling like a worn-out mom or a busy coffee barista; I was a girl on a date, daring her heart to feel loved.

Michael reached over and held my hand.

The American flags hung from every light pole and business. The wind caused the blue and red stripes to wave and greet us. Weeks ago, when the Humvees roared in and the choppers were flying over the town, word had spread about the terrorist's plot to blow up our town. The near-death experience had shocked the town. Patriotism and growth in churchgoing had increased a hundredfold. Prayer meetings where only a month ago just a few elderly members humbly took the time to pray were now filled to capacity. People on their knees, crying out to God, begging for His mercy, protection, and salvation. People were not just saying "God bless America"; they were pouring their hearts and lives out to God.

We wound up at a lovely, quiet restaurant with tables dressed in candlelight and cloth napkins. The restaurant had interior cultured stone walls and lent itself to a bygone era. We sat down, and I just took it all in. This was not the kind of place I would normally take the kids to. We usually pick out a "Here's a red, blue, and yellow crayon. You're welcome to color on the menu" kind of place. The atmosphere here held a quiet, regal state. When the waiter came, I ordered a grilled mountain trout and Michael ordered a rib eye. While we were waiting for dinner to be served, we caught up on the past few days.

"So have you saved the world again while I was gone?" Michael asked.

"Well, only if you count finding Ruston's lost library book, gluing Becca's favorite ballet slipper back together, or getting Mrs. Liddenaul's coffee just right. So…no—not really."

Michael laughed and said, "Actually. All those things you did…those minute, intricate daily moments meant the world to each person you helped."

He got it. I mean, this guy got it. People were "my world." Helping people was the ministry that God had called me to. I think he understood that.

Michael reached out across the table and held my hand.

He looked at me and said, "I've missed you."

"I've missed you too," I said a little shakily.

"I hated being away for even a day, but duty calls. The details of this investigation are ongoing. It will take a while to debrief. In a few weeks, I'll have another weekend free, and then I can come down and spend more time with you and the kids. However, I'll be here through Monday. I'm staying at the local inn," Michael said.

"I'm so glad you are here for a couple more days. What do you say about going to church on Sunday and then doing some sightseeing *Colorado style* on Monday?" I said warmly.

"Sounds like a good deal to me, if the sightseeing involves spending time with you?"

I blinked my "yes." *Yeah, I was "gone" completely and utterly enamored with Michael. This guy is actually good for me. He loves God and is respectful to my family. He has a good job, my dad approves of that. He likes my kids.* A measure of hope filled my heart.

Michael and I walked outside the restaurant after dinner. The restaurant's courtyard was designed with native stone archways and opened to garden paths that had been shoveled. As we walked, holding hands, we talked. I shared about some of my past with Ethan and the troubles that I had experienced.

"Ethan lied to me for years, was unfaithful, and compartmentalized our marriage to a very small section of his life. When Ethan left me for someone else, I lost something of myself: my

lyr title
entire.Lauren Busbee

confidence, my ability to trust, and maybe even a sense of purpose. Time passed before my anger subsided. I still battle feeling down sometimes, and my self-confidence has struggled as well."

Michael's face tensed and then he let out a breath. "Miranda, I can't believe any man would have treated you like that. You are worth more than that. You should be cherished and appreciated." He spoke with truth ringing in his voice.

Michael continued, "I want to tell you about my past, too. I hope—I pray—that you will still want me to be your friend."

I could see that he was preparing me for a painful conversation. I saw a concrete bench supported by an ornate base and sat down. "Michael, whatever has happened, God forgives you. We, as Christians, are all forgiven. We walk in a new life when we seek His love," I said with understanding in my voice.

"I was married before. Right after high school. Her name was Mara. She was a girl who came from a rough upbringing. I wanted to rescue her from it all. She had a lot of emotional problems. Her ability to make friends was difficult for her. I don't blame Mara's inability to trust based on her childhood. I was really focused on my career, though. I was busy moving up in the ranks. I tried to be there for her. She wanted me there with her all the time. We lived at the barracks, so I thought maybe she could make friends with other army wives. Mara misinterpreted their attitudes and believed that no one liked her. She grew depressed and very clingy. I couldn't handle it. I kept withdrawing. Staying busy, I worked through the stress by staying occupied with work and pushing myself past my own abilities to achieve a fair amount of success. I felt like conquering the world was my personal stamp. She started to not trust me.

"When she began accusing me of affairs, she became a very different person that I didn't recognize. We argued when I got word of deployment. She begged me to run away and start new somewhere, but I had my obligations. After I was deployed to Iraq, she wrote me a couple of weeks later, telling me that she made some friends. At the time, I was relieved. I didn't know that she had gotten pulled into the party scene. Before long, I didn't hear from her. I worried about her well-being. She had access to our bank account. One day, all the money was gone. For a month, I didn't know anything.

"During that time I called some friends and family to find out what had happened to her. An army buddy of mine called me one day with word that she had run away to Vegas. She was living with someone else and heavily involved in drugs. I received divorce papers after that. I wish I had tried to help her more, reach out to her, be there for her," Michael's voice broke.

I reached over and put my hand on his arm. I could see that his need to protect was his Achilles' heel. It was both a strength and a weakness. "You can't blame yourself anymore. She left you. You didn't leave her. Maybe you weren't perfect, but nobody is. Michael, your past is a part of you. I'm glad you shared it with me. I just want you to know that I am still your friend."

Michael looked relieved and held me close. "I knew you were special!" he said with a smile.

Michael met us in the church parking lot the next morning. He had been waiting for us by his SUV. My face broke into a huge smile.

Ruston and Becca spoke out. "There's Michael!"

We walked into the church foyer together. It felt like we were a family. Church was a God-glorifying, worship-anointed experience. I loved to raise my hands, praising God for my life and for my family. We went over to my folks for lunch after church.

"I've invited a *few* people to meet Michael, okay?" Mom said.

I walked into the living room and saw Carrie, Scott, the twins, Giselle, Jerome, the pastor, some neighbors I never met..."

"Mom, a *few* people?"

"No time like the present, and besides, I think Michael can handle himself," Mom said rightly as she looked over at Michael mingling on his own.

Michael looked over at me and winked across the room. I walked over and stood by him. This guy was just getting better.

Monday morning came early as I dropped the kids off at school. Instead of driving to work, I drove back to the house. I had told Carrie on Sunday that I arranged for Katy to cover me Monday morning.

"Michael and I are going on another date," I mentioned casually. Carrie had smiled at me in consent. "Enjoy your date."

Chapter 8

My phone rang…it was Michael. "Okay, when does our *sightseeing Colorado style* start?" he asked curiously.

"Our sightseeing is more of a view-finding adventure. How do you feel about skiing?"

"Skiing! I love the idea!" he said enthusiastically.

By nine-ish, we were off. We had decided to rent gear since my skis were in the storage shed and still needed waxing. Thirty minutes later, we arrived at the local ski area and rented skis. We then hit the slopes. The gentle shush of the skis as we flew over the snow sounded like a melody to me. I hadn't skied since last winter. It was exhilarating as I swooped downward. Michael was, of course, amazing on skis. Though I preferred the blues and blue-blacks, he talked me into a black single diamond.

I got to the top of Not Your Friend and hoped that it wasn't an omen. I peered over the edge as my skis partially stuck out.

"Take your time, wide turns," he said reassuringly.

Michael went first, flicking his poles as he went. He stopped midway down.

I leaned forward, planted my pole on the slope below me, and dove down. I managed to make a few turns, athletic-style, hoping he thought I looked confident. Then I hit a sheet of ice. I felt my ski slip sideways and then I tumbled down, landing right in front of Michael.

"Ooooh! Yard sale!" he said as he looked at my scarf, poles, and one ski up the slope.

"You okay?" he said as he wiped off the snow on my goggles with a gloved hand.

I laughed. "I'm fine, really. Just my pride," I said as I snapped my ski back on.

"Actually, you looked amazing, before the fall. You're a really great skier. Everybody hits ice sometime," Michael said, encouraging me. Michael rounded up the other items I had lost, and we were off again.

We were flying fast, and it was really fun. We laughed and chased each other down through the powdery slopes. I had my skiing groove now, and felt I could conquer anything! On the next chairlift ride, I mustered up a question, "Should we try Not Your Friend again?"

"Only, if you want to. I want you to feel comfortable on the slopes we ski. I'm really sorry that I pressed you earlier when—"

I interrupted Michael. "No, I want to do it." I spoke with a confidence that I knew was in me. That adventurous girl that had been, perhaps suppressed for a while. "Let's do it!"

This time, I got right to the top, tipped my skis over the edge, and swooshed down in smooth, fast turns.

"Whew!" I did it and, I beat Michael down! He skied down next to me and did a hockey stop finish. The snow showered lightly on my ankles of my skis and boots. We smiled at each other.

"You're really good. I like those snow curves you made," Michael said with a smile.

The ski trail continued to the bottom, but Michael stopped me from continuing just yet.

"Wait, before we go down, let's enjoy this view."

It truly was incredible. The panorama spread to a view of distant mountains and a frozen lake. The trees all around looked frozen in time. Each branch had snow thickly layered on it. I imagined God icing each branch intricately with the snow, just for our enjoyment.

Michael then leaned over, wrapped his arms around my waist, and kissed me, very tenderly. I felt my body relax with a sigh as our beating hearts were so close to each other. My hands wrapped around his neck as he pulled me closer. "I'd been wanting to do that ever since I met you," he said.

"I had been hoping you would, too." The kiss was perfect.

We skied down and chose the double lift up again.

"So when did you start to like me?" I asked after we settled onto the cold metal seat.

"Well, probably the moment you were silently getting your friend to tell me to take your tent down."

"Oh, it's like that, huh?" I said mischievously.

"I was actually trying to get my head on straight until I saw your bright blue Jeep zooming down *my* road in the National Park. I had to stop you so I could see you again," Michael bantered.

My eyes went to a squint. "But you were so gruff with me," I said, trying to shame him a little.

"I didn't want you to know how I felt about you. The terrorist chatter had increased, and I was trying to stay focused. I just wanted everyone to be safe."

I looked at him, my golden brown eyes glistened slightly with unshed tears. "So how do you feel about me now?" I asked.

Michael reached for my face and tucked a curl under my hat. "How I feel? I love you. I was lovestruck the moment I saw you," he said, gently touching my face with one hand.

"You were?" I said in wonder.

"How do you feel about me?" he asked hesitantly, searching my eyes.

I swallowed and said, "I was in love with you the minute that wet ranger hat showed up at my campsite. You swept my heart up in a hurry, and I haven't stopped thinking of you since."

Michael kissed me again until we realized the lift had stopped. I looked up to see two ski lift attendants laughing at us by the lift hut.

"If you guys are finished, we are going to start the lift again."

We both stood up and skied down.

"I didn't even hear the machinery as we entered the hut?" I said with pink cheeks.

Michael wasn't worried about it. "I'm sure it happens all the time. Why do you think the lifts start and stop so much?"

I laughed as we skied over to the large trail map.

"Should we take Winter's Hue or Runner's End," Michael pondered.

"Let's take Runner's End, ski over to this lift, and try Whiteout?" I suggested.

"You ready for a challenge?" Michael said, noting with his glove the first portion was a double diamond.

"I think I can do it," I said with a nervous laugh. "I'll take it slow and not get out of control." I wondered if I would have to slide, hockey stop style if it's more than I could handle. I'll probably be down on my bum after the first few moguls anyway. The negativity in my head pulled me down. I shrugged my shoulders and stretched my calves in my boots.

Michael looked over at me and said approvingly, "You've got this. I've seen you ski."

I was encouraged and felt light as air as we swiftly glided down the slope.

As we grabbed the middle beam of the small chairlift, I felt my body bounce down and then project forward on the seat. I hung on tight as my skis dangled freely.

"These smaller lifts are an adventure. I think the quad chairs, with their padded seats and footrests, have spoiled me."

Michael laughed. "Where's your alpine spirit? The lifts in the 1940s were a little like these and ring true to a noble ski era. The original ski lifts were tow ropes, then a single chair was created. However, I'm glad a double was later produced," Michael said as he looked over at me with a wink.

The lift slowed to a stop. We were in the middle of the line. I felt a strong gust of wind howl down the mountain, tugging my skis down. This lift did not have a safety bar. I fought to keep myself perched on my seat while one hand held the middle bar and the other held my poles. As I looked down, we were above a steep double-diamond slope. We were also at the edge of this mountain, so I tried not to visualize myself hurtling downward. The slope was completely carved in giant moguls. It looked like an egg crate topper my mattress had on it. The wind carried snow. Beautiful, intricate snowflakes poured down steadily until we were covered in white. I studied the ones on my black ski pants, shining like crystal stars. My skis crested with small, white mountains of snow. I knocked them together and watched the snow fall down.

I didn't like the harsh wind and cold, but on the bright side, at least my visibility had lessened and I couldn't see the bottom anymore. Michael looked over me and seemed a little tense himself. We had been stuck for over twenty minutes.

Michael said, "Let's pray. Father, we want to be safe and we ask that You would help the lift operators to get this lift moving again. I thank you..." He cleared his throat as his emotions washed over him, "I thank you for Miranda and what she means to me. She is my gift and my heart."

A few moments later, we heard the whir of the motors in the distance and the cables above our heads began to move. We both smiled and I heaved a big sigh of relief.

The ski resort was not heavily crowded today, especially on this side of the mountain. Locals usually came on the weekends, and it was still early in the season for a ton of visitors. We arrived at the lift hut, where it looked like one lonely attendant stood warmly inside. We waved a hand of thanks as we slid down the snow-covered ramp.

"This is probably our last run for the afternoon," Michael said.

"I'm just glad the lift operator ran the ski lifts all the way through," I said with relief.

Since we were so near the top of the peak, the snow was dense in form as it snowed down on us. There was no time to dillydally. We saw the sign for Whiteout and trekked over to the edge.

"Ready?" Michael said.

I nodded with a chilled shiver.

The first part of the slope slightly concaved into itself. It wasn't a complete bowl, but its shape added to the challenge. Michael found a line of sight and plunged down expertly, carving turns that looked effortless. I said a prayer and aimed my skis in his direction. The swoop of my skis barreled down hard. I could feel my skis threatening to slide as I hit an icy ridge. I bent my knees and maintained the same direction. I then reached my pole out and planted it for several well-aimed turns. By the time I made it to Michael, I was athletically skiing with a speed and agility that was rewarding and exciting.

The late afternoon sun, rimmed in countless layers of whipped air and snow clouds, momentarily peeked through as we skied our way down the slopes to a mid-point lodge located atop of many popular blue runs. I saw a sign that beckoned me with the words "WARM FOOD." We pressed down on our bindings with our pole tips releasing our boots from the skis. Then we looped our poles with our skis and leaned them outside on the ski rack. Clomping our way inside, I saw a fireplace roaring in the middle of the room.

"Do you mind if I go warm up?"

Michael laughed as he knocked off some piled icy snow from the top of my ski hat.

"You do that, and I'll grab us some food," he said.

I nodded and plunked down, dragging my hats, gloves, and scarf off and laying them on the table. Michael appeared a few minutes later with large Styrofoam cups of hot chocolate, water bottles, hamburgers, and thick-cut French fries.

"Heaven help me, but that looks good!" I said, eyeing the tray.

"What…me? You're glad to see me?" Michael teased as he set the red tray onto the table and shook a little snow from his hat on my now warmed lap.

"That was cold, literally and figuratively!" I laughed.

He sat down with a satisfied smile and held out a hand to me. I reached over and grabbed his warm hand. He prayed over our food with a simple, sincere prayer.

Strong, pure, God-glorifying love. That's what I felt when I thought of our love for each other. I was melting, and it wasn't just from the snow easing off my boots.

I don't know who ate faster. It was like we hadn't seen food in weeks. A few lost French fries lay starkly on my plate. Michael's plate was empty and covered in napkins.

"Thanks, that was wonderful," I said.

"It was just what I needed too. It really hit the spot," Michael said, patting his rock-solid stomach.

We were seated by a see-through fireplace. It had an opening on two sides. Tables were arranged on either side of the huge brick hearth. We gazed at the fire in a fixed contemplation. I'm not sure if the wonderment of the fire was because we were tired, or if the warm flames dancing held us mesmerized with its own merit. The quiet moment allowed me to hear other voices talking in the room. There were more people here than I realized. I guess I had been in my own little world, Michael plus me.

Chapter 9

The people at the lodge sitting at the small round tables were colorful and unique. Some were European, Australian, South American, African, and Asian. Ski resorts were known to draw internationals. I loved that skiing brought the world to common ground. I recognized some various languages spoken: French, German, Spanish and *Arabic...?*

Leaning into Michael, I whispered, "Listen."

"They should be here somewhere. My brothers will be vindicated. Our sources say that they are skiing today."

"We will find them," the other one said menacingly.

"Anyone who betrays my countrymen, betrays Allah."

"Let's separate and take them out," another voice said.

"You will shoot to kill these infidels, named Michael and Miranda, inshallah," a third voice commanded the others.

Michael looked at me as my eyes widened in fear. I quietly translated what I understood. Michael nodded for me to slowly rise. Motioning me to follow him, he pantomimed that we were going to get to the door. I looked back at our table, and the "mom" in me regretted not being able to bus my table. However, the ribbons of fear racing along my arms and neck swung me forward.

A group of European young adults were exiting noisily though the east doorway, the opposite entrance that we came in on. We walked with brisk determination as we joined them, Michael commenting in German about the good ski weather. I kept thinking I should say, "Ja" and "Guten Tag" as possible answers, but thankfully, some of the guys started talking back in German and I was saved from speaking my broken-German nonsense sentence.

Once we walked outside of the lodge, we knew we had to get to the other side where our skis were. We decided to skirt around the back of the lodge. Who knew that we would have to hike in *ski boots*? The lodge was built on a side of a mountain. When the builders constructed the restaurant, half of the building was raised with pilings. This left an opening on the bottom portion. The snow had filled in most of the gaps with great heaps mounted around the building. Michael edged over the snow piles, and we stepped down into one of the gaps beneath the lodge. I felt my shoulder rub against a piling as we hiked lower underneath the structure.

Cross beams were above our heads, causing us to lower ourselves into a hunched walk. Everything felt dark and cold. I pressed my hand on Michael's back, assuring myself that we would stay together. Michael had unzipped his jacket and had his M-9, which never left his side, ready to be drawn.

"See that gap of snow where the sunlight is peeking through," Michael said, quietly pointing.

"We are going to break apart the snow in that thinned-out section and crawl through."

The front of the building was aligned and almost level now. There was very little crawl space left. I slunk down on my belly as Michael did the same and pushed hard, using my feet to propel me forward.

Michael began digging out the snow with his hands as I joined him. The snow was almost ice-packed around the building and seemed immovable. He swung open his serrated blade knife, which was much larger than a pocket knife, and hacked at the ice. Bits of ice crystals spun in, then larger and larger pieces rolled down. I tugged with my hands and broke piece after piece out. Michael picked at the hardened snow forcefully, and his face beaded with sweat. The opening soon became man-sized.

Michael hoisted me up first, and I crawled out. I stayed low while the wind blew snow in my face. Michael emerged a second later and looked around.

I could see it was about fifteen feet to the ski rack. This would be one mad dash to get our skis on and depart. We were about to leave our hiding spot when we saw, coming out the front door, two Arabs. Michael heard my sharp intake of breath. He pressed his finger to his lips, and I nodded. The men walked over to the ski racks and began checking the handwritten names on the temporary stickers that each rental ski had on them. Their backs were turned away from us since they had started at the far end of the racks. We watched them silently. I could see that they were growing frustrated as they roughly threw some skis on the ground.

"Hey, that's mine!" a young man who looked to be in his early twenties shouted, running over.

One of the guys pushed him down face forward, leaving him sputtering snow from his mouth. Michael grimaced and looked angry.

Michael said to me, "Stay down."

Then hurtling across the snow, he manhandled one of the men to the ground. He then wrapped his arm around the guy's neck, squeezing hard, and his body went limp. I saw the other guy pointing a gun at Michael. Michael got off two shots before I saw Michael collapse.

"Michael," I whispered.

In a split second, I considered my options and knew that with my skis close in hand, I could get help on the lower slopes, knowing I would be trapped if I went inside the lodge. Another man spooked me as he came toward me from the backside of the lodge. I ran to my skis, threw them on the ground, clicked into the bindings, and skied off. I could hear my heart pounding in my ears as I raced across the slope. The wind burned my face, whipping my hair. I could tell I was out of control, but I kept on, not letting up. I crossed over through some trees and joined a different trail. I rarely carved a turn as I let my skis stay in parallel form pointed straight to the bottom.

Unable to see clearly as the wind tore the tears from my eyes, I bounced over an elevated ski ramp. I went airborne and landed wildly. My arms and skis sprayed out to gain control. I felt my right knee pulse, and I groaned in pain. I managed to keep skiing and poled faster as I approached a straightaway. Using the last downhill slope to launch myself speedily down, I skied past a quad lift, past the lower lodge, and went straight into the medic station. I literally skied right into the back door. Several red outfitted medics looked at me in surprise, but I began speaking rapidly, panting as I leaned forward in my boots.

I told them of the terrorists at the lodge, feeling adrenaline rush through me with every word.

"Hey, aren't you Miranda Colvin? I read about you in the paper. You're a town hero!"

"The coffee girl," said another. "I read about that."

"Yes, but there won't be a Miranda Colvin or Michael Taylor or maybe even a Mountain View town if we don't stop them," I said with a pleading look.

One of them handed me a cell phone after I requested it while two others began alerting personnel via walkie. The crisis codes for *terrorist threat imminent* went out.

"Level Red confirmed," crackled the walkie in response.

I called General Robert Helding. I had recently memorized his direct line after my mom had made her pumpkin pound cake with cream cheese icing for him. He had told her that he was family now and wanted to visit with all of us again soon.

"General? It's Miranda. They've got Michael. More terrorists have found us. I think the—they've shot him," I stumbled over the words. I hadn't allowed myself to dwell on what I saw. I hoped—*no, prayed*—that I was mistaken.

"Miranda, I'm scrambling planes, helicopters, and ground troops. This will be a massive response. Are you safe?" he asked.

"For the moment," I said tearfully.

"Well then, stay that way," he growled at me and hung up.

A massive evacuation began to take place on the slopes. It wasn't going completely smooth as hundreds of skiers were directed to the parking lots. Many skiers were still on the mountain as the helicopters roared overhead. The medic station became home base. I felt trapped, longing to go back to the lodge and find Michael, but also self-aware that I was needed here. (Besides, no one would have let me go up there anyway.) I focused on camera footage with the security and military personnel. I was the only one who could tell them what the terrorists looked like. Nearby military units deployed onto the mountain searching for the men. The sky turned almost black with all the activity in the air.

Gunfire began filling the air as ground troops met with resistance from the terrorists. I heard a grenade explode, then more explosions. I felt the ground shake as some distant ski lift beams and trees fell to the ground. A second boom went out that caused an avalanche on the upper slopes. The lights blinked then went out as we all ran outside, just in time to see a giant snow mist mushrooming over the mountain.

Later, we learned that the mid-lodge had been detonated when the terrorists pulled the cords on their suicide vests. The ski slopes were in complete destruction as downed trees littered the area. The quad ski lift that went to the upper blue slopes was also partially destroyed. Some cables had popped off the ski lifts that were bringing people down the mountain. A few fell and many were left stranded. I can't say that people weren't hurt, but by the grace of God, broken bones seemed to be the main injuries that were rolling in.

An hour later, I was still helping with triage, offering small amounts of comfort until a nurse or doctor could better address their needs. Several stretchers appeared though the main doors that opened to the slopes, and I shook with recognition at one of the patients. It was Michael.

"You're alive," I shouted as I ran to hold him.

Michael winked at me with his less swollen eye. He looked like the fight had been rough. "I won, you know," Michel said without any bravado sound in his voice.

"What happened up there?" I asked.

"The guy shot me, right here," pointing to a bloody stain leaking through the gauze wrapping his chest. "The bullet missed my heart and arteries by a few inches. I'm glad my heart's okay, because I already gave it to you."

I leaned over and kissed him softly on the lips.

"You may not know this, but after you left flying down the slope, they momentarily focused on skiing after you. I used your diversion and shot off six rounds, taking down one of the guys and wounding the other. I was trying to crawl down the slope when the military arrived and the standoff took place. I wished we could have stopped the detonation from happening." Michael looked pained from the thought. "I'm so glad you made it down," he said to me with a squeeze on my hand. "Seems like we have quite a welcoming party here," Michael said, noting the multitude of army personnel present.

"Your girl, Miranda, got us all in the know after that daredevil ski race she accomplished," a security officer informed Michael. "Plus, she knew the right person to call."

Michael looked at me questioningly.

"General Helding and I are good friends now," I said lightly.

Michael laughed softly and said, "I'm glad you get along with my boss. You did the right thing. This one's going down in the history books!"

Chapter 10

Since that day in the snow, we went on many "regular" dates. Usually with Carrie and Scott or Giselle and Jerome doubling with us. We also spent a lot of time with my family and his. We wanted to make sure that God was in the center of our relationship and maintain a pure focus with accountability. We even met with our pastor, letting him counsel us about marriage, the joys of blending a family, following God, and seeking His direction for our future. I wanted to keep our future on fast-forward, but Michael cautioned me to take our "courtship" slow. This time allowed us to experience God, confirming that He was anointing us with favor and grace. The children were able to adjust and loved Michael too. Ruston respected Michael for the ways that he protected me.

Becca could see that I was glowing with happiness. That made her happy too. She was a good little hugger. She loved to run to Michael when he showed up at the house and wrap her legs around him. "I'm giving you a monkey hug!" she shouted with glee.

Our family had some serious moments too. One evening, Ruston looked at me while in the living room and asked, "Are we safe?"

"Yes, of course, honey. Are you worried about the terrorists?" I asked.

"It's just that it's been two times that some bad guys have gotten close to you. Will they come after all of us?" Ruston asked.

"Do they know where we live?" Becca asked.

"I am glad you asked me about this. Have you been thinking about this for a while?"

"Yeah," they both replied.

"I have tried to protect you from ever hurting in life, but I can't. Life has challenges, like when your dad and I divorced. God has helped you through a lot of ups and downs. I haven't talked with you as much as I should have about all the details of the terrorists. I believed that if we didn't talk about it, you wouldn't worry. Please, know that God will protect you. I'm sorry that you have been feeling scared. Michael is also keeping close tabs on our family. We are going to be safe."

Trusting God was a walk of faith.

Becca came into my room that night wearing a fancy dress-up gown, some sparkly pink wings fringed in a hot pink boa, and a halo, white and fluffy, perched slightly askew on her head.

"Mommy, do you think I'll get to wear a halo in heaven?"

"Darling, I think that what you wear may not be as important as what we do in heaven."

"What are we going to do in heaven?"

"We will sing to God in praise, explore His beautiful creation that He has prepared for us, and we will worship the Lamb who took away our sins. Though we know in Revelation that the church elders had white robes on and golden crowns. So we might wear a white robe. Does that help?"

"Yes. Do you think it will be fun?"

"Honey, heaven will be amazing! Time will feel...different. We can celebrate with God forever. We will feel so loved and full of joy. Imagine the most peace, happiness, and love you've ever felt and that is a glimpse of what heaven is like."

"I think it sounds nice. I wish I didn't have to die to go there!"

"Life is shorter than we really think. Enjoy your life that God has given you. Since you have already asked Jesus in your heart, you know without a doubt that you will be there one day. For now, live for Jesus every day and be kind to others. Did you know that every time you did something unselfish unto the Lord, you are adding a jewel to your crown in heaven?"

"Really! I hope it sparkles a lot!"

"Oh, it will and best of all, we will lay our crowns down in front of our Lord God."

"Well, I hope that my life makes it pretty for Him!"

I hugged Becca on that thought. What a precious heart for Jesus. The Lord must be pleased, I know I am.

"I love you, Mommy."

"I love you too, my little angel."

In late November, we attended Becca's art show at the town library. Mrs. Fogarty had planned a lovely presentation and all the children were so proud. Becca featured her house painting entitled "Our Home."

"Becca, this is going over the fireplace in the living room. I love it!" I said proudly, pointing to her framed painting on exhibit. Ethan had come, which was good for Becca. Though I felt weird introducing Michael to Ethan, I knew they had to meet so I could mentally Twitter off, #heremeetmyexhusband #awkwardmoment.

Ethan actually was nice. Maybe, he felt guilty about everything and wanted me to have some happiness. He had brought a new girlfriend, and they seemed serious. For the kids' sake, I hope they were. Michael was cordial and didn't flinch too much over the meeting. He was pretty loyal to me, so I had prepared him before we had gone to the event, knowing Ethan was coming. Michael had wanted to explain a few things to him about how to respect women and what a good dad was. I had told him that that duty belonged to God. He had agreed to be *good*, mumbling something to God about how his military training could come in handy if need be. I was glad that Michael's words had life and truth. Seeing Ethan made me think of the verse that a double-minded man was unstable in all his ways found in James 1:8.

In December, I longed to see some Christmas miracle in my kitchen. I imagined sugar cookies rolled out in precision and then iced in a decorated dream. I mentioned my cooking woes to Michael and how I had the habit of burning cookies. He surprised me with a cooking class. It occurred on Tuesdays for the duration of three weeks. Christmas cooking was the theme. The third week would include a cooking presentation from all the students and a cookie competition.

I enjoyed the instructors, Harry and Ivy. The husband-and-wife team captured the essence of cooking with love. Humor and practical tips were dispersed regularly as Harry recited their early years in cooking experiences.

"Ah, our beginning was simple, I burned the hot dogs on the grill, and Ivy carefully placed them on the buns."

We all laughed. I related to the burning portion of the story, maybe there was hope for me yet! I thoroughly enjoyed tasting their creations, but my own lacked, shall we say, edibility. My second week helped me build more confidence. My potatoes were creamy, but the gravy was questionable.

"Your combination of flavors was unusual," according to Ivy as she swallowed. "The texture"—indicating the lumps—"needs some work."

I think I'm doomed, I thought to myself.

It wasn't long until the third week came. I was instructed to combine softened butter, powdered sugar, followed by milk and vanilla, with a few drops of green food coloring into the icing. I stirred the bowl too swiftly and clouds of powdered sugar entered my lungs. I sputtered and coughed. I regained what little composure I had left and continued to stir until it was a smooth consistency. After pulling my various Christmas-shaped sugar cookies out of the oven and letting them cool, I spread the green icing onto the wreaths and Christmas trees. *This was it.* I bit my lip nervously as the cookie presentation geared up. Surveying my carefully placed iced creations before the judges, I wondered what they would think.

"Not bad. Buttery, rich, and the icing is very tasty with the vanilla flavoring," Harry said, encouraging me.

I didn't win, but at least my kids could eat the cookies I made. The platter was wiped clean the minute I put them on the counter at home. I had set aside a few cookies for Michael and mailed them to him. He lived an hour away near the army base. Friday evening, he came for a visit.

"Those cookies you sent me were delicious, Miranda. I think you have the hang of it!"

"Well, thanks for the cooking classes. I may have to take the courses offered next year as well," I said gratefully.

"I think it will be well worth it!" Michael said as Ruston high-fived him.

Christmas Eve arrived. I had the presents wrapped and hidden on high shelves in the closets. I had to be very creative because my kids had a "gift sense." I found it uncanny at their lack of desire for surprises. They could "sniff" their way to Christmas or birthday presents like no other children I had seen. Large gifts, like their new bikes were already inside my parents' shed in their backyard. I was certain that I had crossed my Ts and dotted my Is, as far as hiding places were concerned.

The children and I dressed up for Christmas Eve service. I loved Becca's blue velvet dress, black tights, and shiny, black patent leather shoes. Ruston wore his dark brown slacks, a blue button-down shirt, and a plaid tie. I chose a black pencil skirt, midnight blue, silk blouse, and my tall black boots. I know it was silly to have color-coordinated outfits, but I actually thought it was beautiful. Plus, I had reassured Ruston that after pictures, he could take off his tie.

We arrived at church and had my parents take our picture by the outdoor manger scene. Becca loved the way baby Jesus looked so nestled and warm in the hay filled, feeding trough. I took some pictures of her kneeling by the Nativity. She looked very maternal. I felt a connection to Mary and how she must have felt about her child, Jesus. Love swelled in me, and I thanked God for sending Jesus, His only Son.

Ruston swung his arm over my shoulder. "Merry Christmas Eve," he said.

"Merry Christmas Eve to you too. We are going to freeze if we take any more pictures. I'll race you inside the church before the Christmas Eve service begins!"

Becca and Ruston outran me in an instant. Each of us picked out a wax candle with the cardboard cutout underneath from a box in the foyer. Dad, Mom, the children, and I sang many favorite Christmas carols jubilantly. When it came time to light the candles, we circled the room singing "O Little Town of Bethlehem" in quiet harmony and reverence. One by one, the candles were lit by the person next to them. The lights were turned off in the sanctuary as the glow from our candles lit the room.

I was thankful to God for my children and how we could spend Christmas together. Michael was with his family for Christmas Eve and would drive over tomorrow. Ethan was out of town and had asked to keep the kids over New Years. He would give them their presents then. I was so happy to have Christmas Eve and Christmas day with the children.

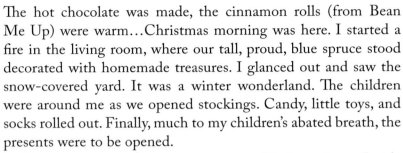

The hot chocolate was made, the cinnamon rolls (from Bean Me Up) were warm…Christmas morning was here. I started a fire in the living room, where our tall, proud, blue spruce stood decorated with homemade treasures. I glanced out and saw the snow-covered yard. It was a winter wonderland. The children were around me as we opened stockings. Candy, little toys, and socks rolled out. Finally, much to my children's abated breath, the presents were to be opened.

Ruston encouraged me to open my gift from them. Inside was a sterling silver necklace that had a cross with a heart in the center.

"Do you love it, Mom?" Becca asked excitedly. Ruston looked anxious too.

"I love it! It's so beautiful."

"Michael helped us!" Becca said, spilling an apparent secret as Ruston shushed her.

"Oh, well, that was nice," I said as I began fishing for details. "When did he do that?"

"He did it when Papa was watching us while you and Gramma went Christmas shopping. Michael, Papa, Ruston, and I went shopping too!"

"It was fun, and we ate corn dogs and French fries," Ruston said.

"Papa said he had fun too," Becca giggled ecstatically.

"He got Gramma a gift," Ruston said with a nod.

"Michael picks out nice gifts too," Becca said softly.

Ruston and Becca rushed at me with information from their pent-up secret-shopping adventure. Turns out I had done a good job of hiding their presents, but so had they! Their secret had kept them too busy hiding their present for me, that they didn't snoop around for their own Christmas presents! We were all surprised that Christmas morning.

Later that day, we drove over to my mom and dad's house and celebrated with them. The children were ecstatic with their new bikes that showed up at their gramma and papa's house. They rode in the driveway for an hour. Ruston built a snow ramp for his bike up to an impressive height. Later, after we went inside to have some Christmas spiced tea, Michael knocked on the door.; I was blown away. This good-looking guy was here, wishing me…

"Merry Christmas!" Michael said, charming me with a smile.

"Merry Christmas, Michael!" I said, giving him a hug. "Did you have a good time with your family?" I asked with joy in my voice.

"It was great. It was nice to slow down and spend some quality time over there. They sent their love. All my family that lives nearby came over to my parents' house yesterday. You know, next year, you are going to have to be there. I kept thinking, *Miranda would love this!*"

I smiled and nodded in agreement. I loved how he threw future words like *next year* around so confidently. My heart sighed in happiness.

Chapter 11

The day before New Year's Eve, my phone rang. Ethan's name popped up.

"Hello. Miranda? Can the kids stay for the whole week? I was working over Christmas and couldn't possibly spend time with the kids. The clients I had were really demanding my time. If I didn't cater to their needs 24-7, I wouldn't have closed the deal. You know how that is?"

No, I really didn't know how that is? Spending time with the kids was a priority for me. I thought with anger. Instead, I yanked out the reply, "Yes, I'm sorry you had to work over Christmas." *Though I hardly doubted it was all work 24-7. Really, that is ridiculous, I know he's lying,* I thought again, annoyed. *Was it really my fault that Ethan worked over Christmas?* His condescension in his voice insinuated that it was.

"Of course, they can stay with you over their entire New Year's break. The kids will enjoy the extra time with you," I said, keeping my voice level. We both had the same idea, that the children being with their dad was a good idea. We just had different perspectives. I wanted the children to have time with their father. I think he wanted it too, but he seemed to be unable to say no to other distractions. He was able to find enough time for other things he enjoyed. I really hoped that the week he spent with the kids was with *him* and not with a sitter like last Thanksgiving.

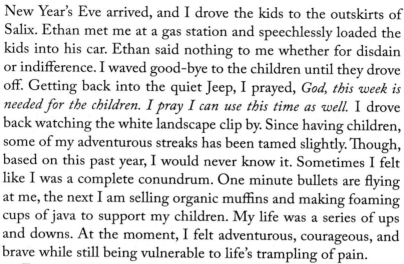

New Year's Eve arrived, and I drove the kids to the outskirts of Salix. Ethan met me at a gas station and speechlessly loaded the kids into his car. Ethan said nothing to me whether for disdain or indifference. I waved good-bye to the children until they drove off. Getting back into the quiet Jeep, I prayed, *God, this week is needed for the children. I pray I can use this time as well.* I drove back watching the white landscape clip by. Since having children, some of my adventurous streaks has been tamed slightly. Though, based on this past year, I would never know it. Sometimes I felt like I was a complete conundrum. One minute bullets are flying at me, the next I am selling organic muffins and making foaming cups of java to support my children. My life was a series of ups and downs. At the moment, I felt adventurous, courageous, and brave while still being vulnerable to life's trampling of pain.

Every so often, like now, I even revisited the feelings of pain the cost of the divorce had on me. Ethan was a force that rendered me tiny. Ethan's shameless lifestyle and attitude made me feel like a speck of dust in his sight. I was once married to him, but now, I was a nuisance and a keeper of his children. I didn't love him, but I should be treated with respect. When did our love die? Probably when I grew busy with the children, overworked by a busy mom's demands. Maybe I didn't take enough time to listen to whom Ethan had met with, or why his brow was furrowed. Perhaps my thighs had too much cellulite, and I needed to jog more. Whatever the reason, Ethan's demise came through stolen moments, a conversation, a joke shared with someone. Eventually, the idea of that person became more intoxicating than my conversation of "What do you want for dinner?" I don't think I meant to lose my "vixen" status of lover and friend.

My real belief, and quite possibly the truth, is that Ethan stopped. He just stopped every part of a husband's job. He stopped caring, he stopped loving, and he stopped yearning to know everything about me. How the curls would spring up tight around my face when it rained. Why I was worried about Ruston's ankle hurting after running. Whether Becca wanted lavender shoe-laces… Silly things, but they mattered to me. After I noticed the changes that occurred, one night I dreamt the children and I were on a lifeboat, but the illusive captain had abandoned our tiny ship for his bigger ship further away. The angry waves swallowed our boat. As we began to capsize, I cried out, but he stared at me, then turned away from the railing. When I awoke, I felt a heaviness settle on me, like I was awarded a plaque entitled "To despair and sadness—may they always be with you."

I have fought that identity. Running to another captain, I ran to Jesus. God answered my cries. He heard my despair.

"Why, my soul, are you downcast? Why so disturbed within me? Put your hope in God, for I will yet praise him, my Savior and my God," as stated in Psalm 33:5. My identity was in Christ, the keeper of my heart. Overall, I have to believe that in this life, the journey and experiences are the gifts that God gives us. He draws us to Himself, whether we are in joy or sadness, and He bears us up under His wings of refuge as we seek Him. We are only stronger in Him because we have eternal hope.

Glancing at the road, then up into the distant sky, I noticed the clouds' white surface hung heavy with snow. It had been snowing steadily for a week. With the disruptive snowfall, I had wondered if traveling today would be wise. The sky looked steel gray with smoky blue trembling ominously in the horizon. I clicked on the radio, and the weather report confirmed my darkening thoughts. We were in for a blizzard. I needed to get home, but first, I would need a few supplies. I knew I was out of batteries and the kids had drunk all the milk this morning. In the midst of my grocery list, I felt a gust blow my car. The wind indicated to me that the blizzard had already started, as it rushed at my Jeep. I adjusted my speed and tried to stay in my lane. The snowflakes were now driving at my windshield, affecting my visibility. Before long, the wind gusts had to be up to thirty-five miles per hour. The snow had fallen so fast I couldn't see any signposts. Drifts of snow covered them.

The taillights of the car ahead of me was all I could see. Unexpectedly, a truck lumbered past me, causing a complete whiteout as his tires kicked up the powdery snow onto my windshield. I knew I couldn't stop, or someone would hit me from behind. I slowed to a crawl, watching ahead for the car in front of me. I spotted the car as it was trying to exit. He must have seen an exit ramp. I wondered if I should get off or keep going. I literally couldn't see a quarter of a mile down the road. I decided to continue, barely going twenty miles per hour.

I felt ice under my wheels as a lack of traction slid my Jeep to the shoulder. I pulled further off the treacherous roadway, with the passenger side hugging a snowbank.

"I know they are here somewhere…" I murmured to myself as I searched deeply into my huge duffel bag. "Snow chains!" I cried out exultantly.

Unzipping the battered yellow pouch, I buttoned my coat and opened my door. Though some people insisted that snow chains were not necessary for a Rubicon, in these blizzard conditions of heavy snow and ice, it was absolutely essential. Laying the chains flat in the front of each tire, I spread them out on the shoulder. I got back into the vehicle and slowly pulled forward, hearing the jingle of the chains and feeling the bumpy lift. Leaning my shoulder into the door as I opened it again against the wind, I completed securing the chains on the tires. Having the heavy V-bar chains on may have slowed my travel speed, but I felt safer. The traction was better, and I drove for another ten miles.

An instant later, I saw cars ahead of me slide into one another. The ice-packed road had rendered their brakes useless. I heard breaks squealing and metal grinding. Immediately, I pulled over again onto the shoulder. In the distance, I saw a red car wedged underneath a pickup truck. A van was locked with a crunched SUV, like a train on one long track. I dialed 911 and was assured that emergency personnel were on their way. I got out to check on the passengers directly in front of me. The mother in the driver's seat looked scared. The kids in the back were young, both still in the car seats.

"Is everybody okay? No injuries?" I asked.

"We're fine, I think, just a little sore from my seatbelt tightening when I slammed on my breaks. I am amazed we didn't hit the car in front of us. Thankfully, we weren't going fast. I was picking them up from daycare on my way home from work. We were almost home, now this!" The woman started to cry.

The little boy and girl in the backseat were already terrified. I tried to comfort the children and offered to pray with the mom. She held my hand, and we prayed.

A state trooper pulled up a few minutes later and began sorting out the mess.

"The interstate is now closed. We will try to get emergency vehicles through, but most of these cars are totaled," the trooper said, noting the ten car pileup.

People with medical issues were evacuated first. Ambulances, police cars, and fire trucks were on the scene. A few tow trucks arrived, but the city was scrambling to locate a few more. After we had already been stuck for an hour, I walked over to the trooper and talked to him for a moment. He glanced at my Jeep and gave me a nod. I walked back over to the mom and her kids and told them some good news!

"The trooper said that since my Jeep was prepared for icy travel, I could leave. Do you want me to transport you and the children as well?"

The mom readily agreed, knowing full well that her small vehicle was no match for these conditions. The children were so agitated by now, I think she had started to lose her mind.

The mother began to pull her car onto the shoulder when her engine died.

The woman opened her car door and walked over to the state trooper who was coordinating the rescue operation, "Add my car to the tow truck list," she said. "My car won't start. I'm getting a ride with...a friend."

The state trooper acknowledged her with a nod and gave her some information. The woman thanked him then leaned against the wind and came back over to me.

"I'm Elisia, by the way. Just give me one more sec. I have to leave my key in the ignition according to the state trooper so that the steering won't lock when the tow truck driver comes to haul off my car."

I turned my Jeep back on, adjusting the heater so it could radiate around then went back to get the kids and relocated their car seats to my Jeep.

We had to wait until the trooper signaled us to leave. I turned the car off then on again in order to not waste gas. Cars, semis, and other vehicles were stacked in the lanes behind me. Soon, the trooper began to direct us, and we began driving around the accidents. Earlier, I had reached into my duffel bag and had given the children some snacks and drinks. They had enjoyed the refreshments and their mom, Elisia, was beyond grateful. I told them about myself and my children. "Mom to mom," we could relate to one another and felt connected. Our bond grew closer as it turned out she was a Christian. They had recently moved to the area and were just beginning to get settled.

"I haven't met very many Christians here. It is really discouraging," Elisia said.

I told her about our church in Mountain View, a twenty-minute drive from where they lived.

"I may like to visit there, we haven't settled on a church yet. I think I long for the connections we used to have. When you walk into a church as a stranger, you feel like you're welcome but..." her voice trailed off.

"I understand, until you get involved, you feel like an outsider, wondering if they might become your friends," I said compassionately.

"Exactly! I know that if I visit God's Mountain View Church, I have one friend," Elisia said warmly.

"Yes, you do, you sure do!" I said, agreeing with her.

I reached her exit a mile later, and she showed me where her neighborhood was. The children were excited as they saw something familiar.

"We are almost home, babies!" Elisia said, relieved.

Pulling into her driveway, Elisia's husband, who had gotten home already, came out to unload the children and help with the car seats.

"A warm bear hug for you and you—grrrr!" he said as he hugged them playfully.

The children squealed in delight. Elisia and I hugged with the understanding that we would be in touch. She had texted me her number so I could save it in my phone. I was so happy that they were safely home, but now, my own journey needed to continue.

"Are you sure you don't want to stay with us?" Elisia asked with concern in her eyes.

"I really need to get home, but thank you, good-bye for now!"

I wanted to be in my own bed and get a few things done before the kids came back. Not that they were coming home soon. Good thing Ethan had planned to keep them for a week. They started school next Monday, so I had said it would be okay. They had looked forward to hanging out with their dad for so long. I knew that County Road 42 was probably passable with my snow chains. My tank had gas, and I felt prepared. I lived just twenty minutes from here, surely it wouldn't take me too long. I drove slowly, feeling the crunch of the snow and hearing the clinkety-clank of the chains.

Plus, we had dogs now. I am still in a bit of shock about the new members of our family. A brown lab and a golden retriever were given to us right after Christmas. One dog was seven and the other was five years old. They had needed to go to a loving home after a mishap or two with their previous owners, according to a friend from church. Though, I didn't need any more responsibility in my life, the dogs needed a home. They were a good fit, and the more I thought about their melty brown eyes and their wagging tails, the more I longed to get home. I urged my car forward. The other part of my brain wondered how my basement looked. I had put them down in the basement with warm blankets and filled their food and water bowls before I left. I could just imagine how bored they have been. What antics were they up to? I sped up, thinking about the possible mess.

A second later, I felt the vehicle slide on some ice. I took my foot off the accelerator and pressed down on the brake. I steered left then right, trying to correct the slide. The ice in this section was so slick that I felt the Jeep drift into a deep snowbank. Trying not to panic, I shifted forward to reverse. I pressed the gas and could hear the whir of the tires attempt to back up. Snow spun behind me in an arch. I prayed a little prayer to God.

Help me, Father, for I'm in trouble—again. Sometimes trouble is the opportunity for me to draw closer to Him. However, I know He is always with me. A verse from James 4:8 came to mind, "Come near to God and He will come near to you…"

Thank you, God, that you are here in this Jeep. Please help me get out this! I tried again, accelerating slowly. The wheels turned backward, and I could see the snowbank moving further away from me. Yippee—I was free! I breathed a sigh of relief, shifted into second, and pressed the gas cautiously. I needed to go slower and pay more attention.

The snow was thick and covered the road. Snow still poured from the sky, letting my wipers swipe furiously against the wind. The trees along the road gave me a border. I drove in the middle, hoping to see some snowplows soon. As I neared our town, an hour later, I was relieved to see that Mountain Vista Road, the main street through town, had been cleared. Sand had been sprinkled liberally creating great traction. I left the chains on until I got home, just because I was apprehensive about getting to Bowie and Maui as soon as possible.

I ran inside and scurried to the basement stairs. Opening the door with my senses alert…all was quiet.

"Hey, doggies. You all right?"

They were both sacked out, asleep on my Christmas tree skirt. Three of the six Christmas plastic storage bins had been knocked down and dumped out. Greenery, lights, and bows were twisted in a big knot. Piles of silver ribbons, grapevine, and sparkly ornaments littered the floor. Maui and Bowie's tails began to tap the floor as they slowly stood up, trying to appear innocent.

"Oh, you know nothing about this, right?" They both ran over to me and licked my hands. "All right, all right, I forgive you. But this can never happen again. No, no!" I said sternly, pointing to the messy piles. Both seemed to look at me in understanding. Dogs were really good at looking cute and vulnerable. I would have to clean this up tomorrow. "This will be a long project," I said audibly with a sigh.

"Let's go outside, and you two can get some energy out." The winds had died down slightly, but it was still snowing. They jumped in the deep snow, disappearing for a moment, then ran back inside the house. I was glad to have us all inside. I texted the kids, and they said they were safe. By that evening, we were all snoozing in the living room. I had a chenille throw and an overturned book on my lap while the dogs stayed warm by the fire on the rug. "I am glad you dogs are *so* at home here." Maui perked up her ear as Bowie yawned. They were content and so was I.

Chapter 12

In mid-January, Michael and I took a walk on a frozen lake outside of town. Work had kept him busy, and we had hardly seen each other since Christmas day. We set off in the direction of the island. I timidly set my feet on the ice. I jumped back as I heard a sinister jolt under my feet. The cracking of the ice alarmed me, but Michael assured me that the lake was frozen, but the currents below caused some movement in the ice. He held my hand as we walked. The wintry tundra stretched for miles. I saw white ice and snow in every direction. The sun peeked out for a moment and suddenly the gray day, dazzled the ice and awoke the diamonds that had been hidden in the dullness. I caught my breath and appreciated that the day was anything but ordinary.

I cleared my throat. "Michael, a long time ago Ethan called me *normal.* I'm sorry to mention his name, but his words cut me from within. To him, I was a run-of-the-mill, commonplace, traditional, and average woman. How do you see me?"

"Oh, Miranda. You are anything, but normal. The fact that you are a mom to two extraordinary kids is testimony of that. Also, I've seen you conquer extreme odds as you raced on skis to save a town. You climbed a mountain against impossible odds. Your commitment to God is beyond anyone I have ever met. Normal is not a word in your vocabulary. I would have to call you exceptional and beautiful and amazing and courageous and wise and worth loving..." Michael continued until my heart felt full and spilled over.

We neared the small island in the center of the massive frozen lake. I would be glad to rest, maybe build a fire to warm up and enjoy the beauty and sense of accomplishment of walking so far. However just as I took another step, I heard a crack that echoed off the ice. Slowly, the frozen lake beneath me began to splinter into thin, ragged veins. I stood still, terrified of plunging down and becoming trapped beneath the ice. Michael was next to me, immobilized by the same situation. Water began to seep around the ice.

I prayed rapidly, "God be with us," as I breathed in a panicked breath.

"We are going to run. Don't stop until you reach the island," Michael said as he gripped my hand. "Ready. Go!"

We sprinted to the island, each step breaking the thin ice. I could feel the torn ice clutch at my ankles as I moved briskly to take more steps. Toward the end, my shoes were completely immersed. My ankles felt numb as the wet lake lapped at me. My feet sank lower, icy water hitting my calves. Plunging downward, I gasped in fear, but just then, my feet touched on a wet, shifting layer of ice below the initial surface. Michael yanked my arm, catapulting me up in the air. We then hurtled our bodies the final feet to land on the tree roots that anchored the island. Sloshing up onto land, we sat down, allowing the adrenaline of the moment dissipate into the cold air.

Michael hugged me. "I am so glad you are safe."

"I am glad we both survived," I responded, feeling numb from the cold and shock. "Please tell me that we don't have to walk back," I said as the hopelessness of our situation settled in like the bitter winter chill that had found its way into my bones.

Michael started a small fire with some matches and driftwood he had gathered. I warmed my hands and legs, letting the heat seep some life into my frigid bones. Though the quiet walk on the lake had turned into a nightmarish quality, watching Michael tuck some more branches into the fire stilled my fear. He had been in survival situations before. He had led platoons of men through battle. Getting one cold female back home was probably easier than I could imagine.

Michael looked at me and asked kindly, "Warming up?"

I responded with a nod.

Michael sat down, and we began contemplating our situation. The day was early, so the sun, what little winter sun there was, would be out for a while.

"We could hike back toward the opposite side of the lake and try to find an alternate route back across. I cringed at the thought of putting one more step on the deceiving lake.

"The island tree roots may have weakened the area surrounding the lake, perhaps if we head north, then skirt around in the direction of Mt. Frourio, we will have a better experience on solid ice," Michael said, putting his arm around me. "God is with us. This is just one more adventure for our history book."

I liked the sound of "our history book."

"Stay here a few more minutes while I scope out a good starting point." Michael began walking to the other end of the island. I saw him pick up some sticks and heavy rocks, launching them onto the ice. The rock rolled in triumphant thumps, knocking the branches he had thrown first. "Strike! Hey, Miranda," Michael called, "who says I never take you anywhere? Bowling is fun!"

I laughed at the expression on his face. Boys will be boys! "So you think it's safe?" I responded uncertainly.

"Yes, I think the ice is going to hold," Michael replied confidently.

A black-billed magpie bird, determined to survive the winter in his home, flew off in a loud flutter of wings above my head. He soared high then lowered his long tail and abruptly landed on the northern portion of the lake. Pecking his beak, he nicked the ice. Though I knew that we were heavier than he, I wondered if he was telling us that the ice was hard. I knew God had used a donkey in the Bible to speak to a man. Maybe God was using this bird to speak to us. I shoved snow over the fire, letting the sizzle and steam vapor abate until it was completely out.

Michael and I began our journey back across the lake. Gingerly, I stepped, fearing to put my weight fully down on the ice. The ice stayed firm, and I walked more confidently. The bird took flight again. I waved a hand of thanks, praising God for His provision from such a beautiful and humble being.

I recited to Michael, "'Look at the birds of the air; they do not sow or reap or store away in barns, and yet your heavenly Father feeds them. Are you not much more valuable than they?' found in Matthew 6:26."

"True, very valuable."

Michael held my hand, and we walked. The frozen lake stayed rock-solid but slippery on the surface. We began gliding, pretending to be ice skaters, twirling in a pair's competition. We reached the shore after walking for an hour. I was so glad to climb into the Jeep and rotate the heater dial to full blast. We picked up the kids at my mom and dad's, sharing with them all the wonders of a day on the ice.

Chapter 13

February blinked by, and March settled in with a barrage of household work. I folded "six hundred" pounds of clothes, made a fruit salad (no cooking involved) for a church get-together, and considered ironing a dress shirt for Ruston. After dwelling on the thought fleetingly, I changed my mind. I knew full well that there is only so much I can accomplish in a day or lifetime for that matter. Ironing was an art form passed down from generation to generation. The stiff, starched shirts, pillowcases, T-shirts, and other paraphernalia that people used to iron was not my cup of tea. It's over my pay grade. Probably because I have so much other stuff to do, like matching socks, working full-time, and washing the dogs.

The thought of the dogs made me remember that they needed a walk. "Come here, Bowie and Maui." Both dogs leapt from their peaceful slumber.

"Kids, do you want to go too?"

"Yeah, let's go!" Ruston said as he threw his wireless controller on the floor, and Becca laid her sketchpad on the table.

Becca unhooked Maui's hot pink leash while Ruston grasped Bowie's blue one from the wall board that also held their backpacks. The dogs were ecstatic as we walked, or rather ran, through the neighborhood, only halting instantly and momentarily when an incredible dog smell hit their long noses.

"Can we run them to the park?" Ruston asked.

"Sure, it's a long way, but why not?" I replied, huffing slightly.

We set off down the hill, passing the neighbors as they worked in their front yards. I waved hi but could not chat as the dogs pulled us forward by another unseen force…more dog scents. This categorically profound phenomena had been unearthed as our location grew closer to the park. Other families with dogs were also running for their lives as we all chased the dog dreams together. In a moment, we arrived at this euphoric moment, when all dogs at the park meet, bark, and sniff. Then we unequivocally ran together in a general relay toward a central large tree that held an unbounded amount of more dog smells. (Our dogs' primary goal was to get to the tree and enjoy its trademark scent. Our family's goal was to survive the run to the tree…if we lasted that long.)

We arrived unscathed at the tree, breathing hard and, albeit exhausted, but happy. That was the epitome of running our dogs in the park!

We had obviously survived as I walked into the house, dragging the leashes that were attached to two worn-out dogs. "Maui, Bowie…here is some water." Their tails wagged as they noisily slurped water with their long pink tongues.

"Mom, can I have some water too?" Ruston asked as he slunk into a chair in the living room.

Becca leaned into a pillow on the couch and said, "Mom, I think I'm more tired than they are."

After bringing cups of water to both of them, I, too, drank a refreshing sip of cool mountain water. One of the things I loved about living here in Mountain View was the taste of the cold, sweet water. I didn't even have to filter it. The water was so fresh and clean.

"So what do you guys think about having two dogs?"

"I love them. They are my best friends!" Becca said, enthused.

"Ruston? What about you?" I asked, nodding my head toward the sleeping pile of fur by Ruston's feet.

Ruston knelt down, burying his hands in Bowie's fur. "I love them too. I feel like they are a gift. I can't imagine our family without them."

"So are you going to take them to the park tomorrow?"

"Absolutely!" Ruston replied with a bit of a grin.

"Me too! Can't wait," Becca said, closing her eyes to rest.

One weekend in April, I took the kids in my Jeep to explore some old mining towns. Michael was scheduled to be down that weekend but was delayed due to work. I knew that we could handle it. I drove for an hour to a small town then turned left onto a gravel road. Signs were limited, but I did have a general sense of where I was going. We traveled up the road at a leisurely pace, admiring the views. Blue skies and tall grass swayed in the breeze. We crossed a small stream. The water splashed up on either side of our Jeep with a swish. The kids laughed. *What a great day!* I thought.

Then the Jeep began to climb upward on a steep incline. As the Jeep slowly progressed, I knocked the gear down to third, letting the Jeep stick hard to the mountain road. I had set the Jeep to be four-wheel drive to have extra traction. There was no guard rails, just a narrow gravel trail. The road became tighter and rougher. We came upon some boulders.

"Here we go, guys."

I pressed down hard on the gas, holding the steering wheel slightly to the left of the mountain. One wrong move and we could hurtle down the side of the mountain. I felt the Jeep launch forward over the rocks. As we cleared the rock section, I saw that a hairpin turn coming at me fast. I jerked the wheel hard to the left and pressed on the gas again. The bumpy rocks and boulders bounced us like a ship on a raging ocean. My palms were sweating and my fingers clenched deeper into the steering well. The Jeep catapulted upward, leaving dust and sliding rocks in our wake.

"You go, Mom!" Ruston said.

Becca looked around nervously as I breathed a prayer of thanks. Maybe this wasn't such a good idea. I thought. However, I maintained a calm demeanor for the kids and said, "We did it!"

Becca looked over at the edge from her seat and could see a lake far below. "Mom, are we going to make it?"

"Of course. This is fun," I said, reminding them and myself. "Just us on an adventure!"

We continued upward, each turn becoming tighter and rockier. The trail became so narrow that I began to wonder if the right side of the Jeep could stay on the trail without slipping.

"Ruston, get out on my side and walk over to the path. Tell me if the Jeep has enough room to go forward."

Ruston began climbing out when Becca wailed, "Me too!" Jumping out on the driver's side, she held Ruston's hand as they both peered at the trail.

"I think you can make it, Mom," Ruston called to me.

Becca looked very small and young, waving and sending an encouraging smile.

"Thanks!" I forced out in a croak. The truth was, I couldn't go back at this point. There was no place to turn around. I just had to go forward. I was basing my life on my ten-year-old son saying, "I think you can make it."

"God, I got myself into this. My intentions were good—family togetherness. What I didn't count on was the danger involved in my 'little adventure.' Lord, give me wisdom and strength. In Jesus' name, amen." Making sure that Ruston and Becca were safe up on the grass on the road above me, I slowly began to accelerate. Leaning my whole body to the left, like I could make a difference, I felt the Jeep pitch forward. Showers of rocks flung themselves to the earth below.

The trail itself looked like it aligned with the far-right headlight. A tight turn was upon me as I swung back toward the mountain. The switchback was full of boulders, causing the Jeep to be at a sharp incline, and I couldn't see above my dashboard. With one final tug on the steering wheel and a hard press on the gas, the Jeep lingered forward then planted itself firmly on smooth road. Becca and Ruston shouted and jumped up and down.

"Yeah, Mom!" Becca shouted.

"Good driving!" Ruston said.

The kids got back in, buckling their seat belts with a decided click to the buckle. I smiled weakly and moved up the mountain. The road widened slightly, and we made it up to the old mining settlement we had been aiming for. I was so glad to park our car in some old civilization. I imagined a man running out of the rickety buildings with a hat, shouting at me for getting such a foolhardy plan in my head. We walked over to some settlement houses, which had, at one time, according to a weather-beaten sign, housed the general manager of the mine with his wife and children. Looking around the old wooden floors, empty fireplaces, and chinked walls, I felt a nostalgic mood settle on me.

A family once lived here. Working and living in some of the harshest of conditions. How did they survive the winters? Were they really happy? I was glad when I came outside again and breathed in the fresh air. A small white flower shook its petals at me against the wind. The flower was happy. It belonged there. Maybe we did not. I felt loneliness sweep over me. The isolation of our location multiplied by the feeling of being "the responsible one" weighed on me. How were we going to get down? With the steep acceleration of the narrow, downhill road; I could only imagine one incredibly scary descent.

I heard, before I saw, as the wind carried a sound of a vehicle. A road that I had not seen earlier contained a familiar SUV on it.

"Michael!" I breathed a sigh of relief.

Mom and Dad got out of Michael's SUV too and the kids starting laughing with happiness.

"We found you! You mentioned you were going to this mining camp in your Jeep, so when Michael called looking for you... well...the plan came together to meet you up here!" Mom said.

"What road did you take to get here?" I questioned, feeling hopeful.

"We came up on a lovely scenic highway that Michael found in an information book he had purchased."

"A scenic highway? So you're saying we can drive home that way?" I asked, feeling my hands unclench in relief.

Michael walked over and hugged me. "Of course, which way did you come? Is there another way? Do you want to go back that same way?"

The kids and I looked over at each other and laughed exuberantly. Our own miracle had occurred that day, not only had we survived me driving a crazy road, but we had become a closer family. We needed each other. Our family togetherness was bridged by God. He had a way of blending families that was in it of itself a gift. The kids relayed all the adventures we had experienced. Michael and Dad got out a Jeep trail book and found a thin squiggly line that we had gone up. Turns out, I had gone up an old Jeep trail that was no longer in regular use and hadn't been maintained.

Michael said he would even drive my Jeep on the way home down the highway to give me a break, and the kids could ride back with Gramma and Papa. I loved the idea of just enjoying the views and riding with Michael. The adventure had turned itself around, thanks to God and my loving family!

I knew my guardian angels were relieved since they had held the Jeep the whole way up here. "Thanks, guys, I know I can be a lot of trouble, especially lately!" I winked out at the heavens, feeling grateful that I wasn't alone in this universe. I know there is so much more on this earth. "For our struggle is not against flesh and blood, but against the rulers, against the authorities, against the powers of this dark world and against the spiritual forces of evil in the heavenly realms" (Ephesians 6:12).

The ruins were no longer sad now. I felt safe, and the beauty and memories captured in the settlement was an idyllic setting. It was a perfect spot for the extravagant lunch of pecan and grape-laden chicken salad sandwiches, fresh strawberries, and home-made chocolate chip cookies that Mom brought!

As Michael drove, we talked about all the wonderful experiences that we would like to share together. One day, we could have a life together. We dreamed of our home, our lives becoming one. I was even tempted to mention a honeymoon destination, but that probably needed to be discussed later.

Michael opened up about all his travel with the army. He had been to so many amazing places. However, some of those places I thought would not be very fun to visit. He kept the conversation light, rarely touching on the guys he'd lost, the wars he'd seen, or the poverty he'd observed. I'm sure some of what he'd seen couldn't be talked about for security reasons. However, I hoped that one day, he could unfold the parts of his life that had caused him pain. From what I understand, once you've seen war, you are not the same, and talking to a civilian about combat can seem uncomfortable. Nevertheless, he did tell me a little about his re-acclimation to everyday life.

Michael began, "When I first got back from Iraq, I couldn't handle hearing any fireworks or gunfire in hunting season. I was so on edge for my first Fourth of July party, that's when my mom touched me on the back of the shoulder, I threw my plate in the air and dove under the picnic table. I can joke about that now, but at the time, my heart rate stayed high, and my sense of alertness was channeled so completely that I had to leave the party.

"That night, I just drove and drove. I wound up at an army friend's house a couple hours from my hometown. He told me that it was normal what I was going through. It would take time, but eventually, I could adjust to civilian life. I thank God for the people that He brought into my life to encourage me. I'm better now. I can set off fireworks with the best of them!" Michael said as I smiled, thinking that Ruston would love that.

Getting to know someone, truly taking the time to understand what was underneath his heart; I needed to do this and wanted to. Sure, I was in love with Michael, and I knew that he loved me. I also knew that I had to make the effort to be a friend as well. Marriage could be a long ride, if we didn't know what made each other "tick." A friend is someone who "gets you," even on the bad days. As in some marriages, one person's bad day is released on all, causing a chain reaction. I needed to know who he was, how he handled stress, and what his weaknesses were. I wanted to one day walk down the aisle with my eyes wide open.

Chapter 14

I worked late every day this past week and felt unusually grumpy. My parents were out of town, so the kids had to stay in the extended aftercare at school. I didn't know those workers, and I think they were always ready to go home. They made me feel judged and alone as they stared at my frizzy hair and smudged mascara one evening. I guess I was a few minutes late because they reminded me of the late charges fee and then locked the doors of the school as we left. Then they walked out with us to their cars. Their inner thoughts spilled out through their eyes: "She is so disorganized and scattered. She looks tired. Her kids have been waiting for her. They need some attention." Every critical thought pulsed through me and reiterated a feeling of isolation.

That feeling compounded when we drove to the library as we returned some overdue library books. The librarian clucked her tongue and squinted her eyes at me when Ruston and Becca starting playing chase between the shelves. They were out of control tonight. I was so annoyed with the children, and very tired. When we arrived home, their clothes were everywhere. Feeling short-tempered, I whipped around the house latching onto runaway socks, dirty clothes under beds, and backpacks tumbling out on the floor.

"Y'all really need to help me more. Everything is a mess, and I didn't do all this," I said loudly with angry tears glinting in my eyes.

"Mom, don't be mad," Ruston said, trying to help pick up.

"Yeah, Mom, I'm sorry, I want to help too," Becca said with a sniffle.

I froze for a moment and looked at their big eyes. "Look, I'm sorry I lost my temper. I just feel overwhelmed sometimes. Help me get this stuff sorted and in the washer," I said with my arms full of clothes.

That's when it happened. I slipped in a pool of water in the doorway off the laundry room.

"Ack! Why is there water everywhere?" I said, yelling and then promptly burst into tears.

"Mom, Mom, what's wrong?" Becca came running over.

"Water...everywhere...why?" I said, sobbing and sputtering. Putting my hand in the water, I stood up, completely soaked as droplets of the cold liquid continued to course down my pant legs.

"We need a new washing machine," I said in a glum voice. "We can't afford that."

"God will provide, Mom. We have to trust God and wait on Him," Becca said with wise, Spirit-filled words.

"From the mouths of babes. Honey, you are right. God will provide," I said, hugging her. I wanted to give Ruston a hug, but I didn't see him.

"Where's Ruston? Ruston, honey, where are you?" I said as I looked in the kitchen.

"Okay, thanks, bye." Ruston grinned as he looked over at me and clicked the phone to *off*.

"Who was that on the phone?"

"It was Michael."

"You called him?"

"No. He called here. You probably didn't hear the phone ring with all the well, you know, crying and stuff."

"You told him I was crying?"

"Well, he could hear it in the background. You were pretty upset."

"Oh," I said, wiping my cheeks.

Ruston hugged me and said, "It's all right. Michael knows what to do. He's coming over."

"He is?"

"Yeah, and he's going to take a look at the washing machine," Ruston said kindly.

"Right now?"

"Right now," Ruston said, patting my back.

Michael came over in less than an hour.

"You got here fast," I said, opening the door, mop in hand.

"Hey, I'm glad to be here and help if I can," Michael said, giving me a hug.

He got right to work, unscrewing the front of the washing machine with his tools. His jeans and old T-shirt was a comforting sight. Just having a man around the house to do fix-it projects was a mental break.

"Looks like the bottom's rusted out. How old is this machine?"

"It came with the house, so *old*."

"Looks like I get to buy you a big, metal, square cube today."

"Michael, you don't…" My arms fell to my side.

Michael was nodding and said, "Yes, I do."

My new washing machine was a quiet blend of technology and top-of-the-line features. I purposefully shoved more jeans into the tub, delighting in its huge capacity.

"Michael, I can't thank you enough."

"Well, how about a kiss right here?" tapping his lips with his index finger.

I kissed him in happiness. It was a long dream of mine to have a man who went the extra mile and sought to provide gestures of love that I actually needed. I'm not saying that flowers and chocolates would be unappreciated, but sometimes, a washing machine is a bouquet when you are a single mom scraping by.

"If an army marches on its stomach, a family marches with clean clothes. So thank you!" I said.

"Speaking of armies marching on its stomach…why don't I take everyone out to a late dinner?" Michael said.

"Mexican food, please," Becca called from the living room.

I laughed. "Were you eavesdropping?"

"Well, I was getting very hungry," Becca said as she rubbed her tummy.

"Well, you shall not be hungry anymore, let's go have a fiesta!" Michael swooped Becca up onto his shoulders and called to Ruston, "Fiesta awaits!"

The waiter came to the table.

"We're having a fiesta party," Becca said with enthusiasm.

"Oh, and who are we celebrating today?" the waiter queried.

"Not who, a what. We just got a new washing machine," Becca said innocently, nodding.

"A what?"

"A washing machine. The one we had before dumped like a thousand pounds of water into the house," Ruston told the waiter.

"Oh, well, this is a cause for celebration! I say, ice cream on the house!" the waiter announced to our table with a bow.

Becca laughed and clapped her hands. "My tummy already says, 'thank you!'"

I squeezed Michael's hand in thanks as I bit a savory chip dipped in fresh salsa.

Chapter 15

Saturday at 3:00 p.m., my phone rang with its short, digital melody of "Amazing Grace." The screen read Carrie Thompkins.

"Carrie?"

"Hi, Miranda…I have a huge favor to ask of you. The twins' babysitter was supposed to watch the children tonight, but she's not feeling well. She offered to keep them still, but I thought of you. Would you mind terribly, if they could come over and stayed for about four hours?"

"Casey and Stacey are more than welcome to come over. We'll order pizza, watch movies, and play games—it will be fun!"

"Oh, thanks, Miranda. Scott and I really need to have this date. We haven't been out since our anniversary, which was around Christmas."

"We are happy to do it. Michael may swing by, so it will be a merry time!"

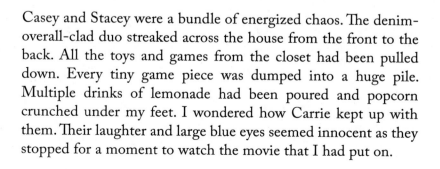

Casey and Stacey were a bundle of energized chaos. The denim-overall-clad duo streaked across the house from the front to the back. All the toys and games from the closet had been pulled down. Every tiny game piece was dumped into a huge pile. Multiple drinks of lemonade had been poured and popcorn crunched under my feet. I wondered how Carrie kept up with them. Their laughter and large blue eyes seemed innocent as they stopped for a moment to watch the movie that I had put on.

Whew, that's a relief! The movie must have caught their interest as I noticed them settling down onto some overstuffed pillows strewn across the floor. I used the moment to sweep the kitchen floor with all the popcorn debris. Next, I sat down with Michael as we sorted some spilled game pieces, fake money, playing cards, plastic purple ponies, some dolls, and a bucket of cars that had been Ruston's. I reached under an armchair for some lose checkers and pulled out some unmatched socks.

"So that's where you've been hiding," I mused. Walking to the laundry room, I tossed them in the dirty clothes hamper then continued on my journey of organization. I sorted some toppled children's books and placed the last plastic container filled with toys back on the shelf.

"Amazing, isn't it? So cute yet so destructive?" I said, remembering Ruston and Becca being this little.

"Did your kids have the same tendencies?" Michael asked curiously.

"Oh yes. They weren't perfect at the age of three. They're not perfect now, but they have matured some. They've learned how to participate in my whirlwind-company's-coming cleanup projects. They still make a mess on a daily basis, but we are making strides with responsibility."

The movie ended, and Michael flew the children around the room like a helicopter. Casey and Stacey went first, making *chop-chop-chop* noises with their hands. Becca went next, squealing with delight. Ruston watched, being cool and laid back until Michael grabbed Ruston and piggybacked him in a gallop through the kitchen and living room. The goofy smiles on their faces were priceless.

"How were they? Not too much trouble?" Carrie asked seriously when she and Scott returned.

"No, no trouble at all. They can even come back some time," I said, smiling.

"Oh, Miranda, you are a good friend!" Carrie said knowingly.

"No, really—they are good kids, and just look at your countenance. You look happy and so in love with Scott. It's worth it—to see that again on your face."

"I have to admit, an uninterrupted dinner with my husband was sublime. Maybe I can watch Ruston and Becca one night next weekend, so you and Michael can have a date?"

"Sounds great!" hugging her good-bye.

"Whew, I'm beat!" I said to Michael as I closed the front door. "Ruston, Becca, time to get ready for bed."

"Is Michael staying over too?" Ruston asked.

"No, Michael doesn't do that," I answered.

"Well, how come Daddy's girlfriend always does?" Becca asked with an innocent blink.

"Come here, both of you," Michael said, pulling them onto the couch.

"I care about your mom very much. I also respect her and the ways of God. The Bible encourages a man to marry a woman before he stays overnight with her. That's the godly way of living. It saves a lot of heartache too. Plus, God blesses our special relationship. You want God to bless us, right?"

"Yeah, I do."

"Me too!"

"Does that mean Dad isn't blessed by God?" Ruston asked with a sincere look on his face.

"Ruston, unfortunately, your dad has made choices in his life that does not please God. It's the same way with us. We all make mistakes. Sometimes we are not obedient. A habitual sin, the kind of sin you do over and over again, leads to destruction. I pray your dad starts to make better choices for his sake and yours. You can pray for your dad right now, if you want."

"Dear God, I pray my dad makes better choices so he can be an example to us. In Jesus' name, amen." Ruston's sweet, sincere prayer was echoed by Becca's "Amen." Tears sprang to my eyes as I thanked God for Michael turning their questions into a teachable moment.

Becca's recital was scheduled for mid-May. I received a text two days prior from Ethan.

"Can you tell Becca that I can't make it to her dance thing? Work stuff, you know."

"No, I can't. You will have to tell Becca yourself. This is a promise between you and her. Just remember, she has been practicing all year and is expecting you. Prioritize them like you would a VIP," I texted back.

Five minutes passed, and my phone buzzed.

"I will get back with you," Ethan responded.

Another day went by and my phone rang; Ethan's name was on the screen.

"I'm planning on coming to the recital."

"Becca will be very happy to see you. It's about the kids, Ethan. That's what I care about," I said matter of factly.

"I know, and I appreciate what you do for them," Ethan said in earnest.

I was surprised to hear praise from him. *That's unusual,* I thought to myself.

"I'm bringing someone with me," Ethan interrupted my thoughts.

"Oh."

"My fiancé."

"Wow, okay, that's...well, uh, good for you," I stammered.

This was it, the final coffin. The death of our marriage was two years ago, but the funeral felt like today. My heart hammered within me and I kept thinking, *I hope she's nice to the kids.*

Ethan answered my thoughts. "She loves kids. She has a lot of nieces and nephews. In fact, she works with kids."

"She does?"

"Yeah, as a model. Sometimes she poses with children in the magazine's spread."

I wanted to say, *Wow-wee, that makes her an expert.* However, I held my sarcasm and said, "She sounds nice." I was relieved that my voice sounded relaxed, almost pleasant.

"Okay, well, bye," Ethan said, hanging up.

I told the kids the news about their dad. They weren't totally surprised. In fact, they said she had already moved into their dad's apartment. Ruston told me that she had a lot of pillows, candles, pictures, clothes, and shoes. I would be amazed at the amount of shoes, he had said to me rolling his eyes and spreading his arms out in proposed measurement. My kids were amazing how God enabled them to flow with life's waves. I hugged them and prayed that God would be with us in the days ahead.

Mom called me an hour later.

"Your voice sounds tight, are you all right?"

"Yes, I'm fine. I just, well…Ethan called with some interesting news—he's engaged."

"Miranda, that's a good thing. Maybe it will settle him down and give the kids some more stability."

"I know, but the kids are going to have a stepmom. That affects the kids."

"Miranda, you've trusted God in the past, you can trust God in your children's future too.

"You're right, I can't control this."

"No, you can't. However, you can control where you put your worry."

"Worry has a destination?"

"God's hands are where you place worry every time you pray," Mom said wisely.

She was right. Praying to God gave me peace as I let the situation lift into His loving hands.

Becca did amazing in her recital. Her costume, which was covered in pink and purple sequins, seemingly lit up the stage. We were all sitting on one row: my mom and dad, Michael, Ruston, Ethan and Sahara (Ethan's fiancé.) Her skinny arms linked in Ethan's tightly. Their fingers laced with her rock on her left ring finger sticking out. You would have thought the diamond's expanse bridged the distance of the moon from the sun—it was that big. Their hips were glued to one another, since they were sitting so close to each other. I felt annoyed at their presence and wished that they weren't on our row. However, this was about supporting Becca.

I mentally broke the spirit of "judgmental-ness" and focused on the rest of the performance. Michael reached over, held my hand, and winked at me. I relaxed with a sigh. I was so blessed. *Thank you, God.* God enabled me to enjoy the rest of the evening, congratulate Ethan and Sahara without a hint of hypocrisy, and recognize the incredible gifts that were all around me— my family!

Chapter 16

One of my favorite times of the day at Bean Me Up was mid-morning. The older locals would come by to discuss politics and weather over a warm brew of coffee.

"Good morning, Mr. Oaklan. Hi, Mr. Anderson."

Mr. Oaklan was thin and balding, but very tall. His legs looked like croquet mallets, skinny with big feet at the end. He stooped slightly and wore a sweater vest year round. Mr. Anderson, on the other hand, was thick-waisted and had large hands. His long arms were covered in tattoos from his navy days, and even though his wrinkles and veins betrayed his age, he was still strong. Both men were kind and funny.

"Hi there, Ms. Miranda. I heard Ruston beat out Kingston at the meet," Mr. Oaklan conversed.

"Yep, he's going to state," I informed him.

"You youngins sure stay busy. W'all I remember the time when we just ran because we had to stay warm!" Mr. Anderson guffawed at Mr. Oaklan's pun.

Mr. Oaklan continued, "We didn't have central heat. We chopped wood for the one stove in our cabin. Yeah, I guess growing older we have seen a lot of changes. Central heat being one of them. I can't imagine, with my arthritis acting up, that I could do what I did back then."

"Oh, Mr. Oaklan, I'm sure you could put me to shame with all you do around this town," I proclaimed.

"Dearie, that may be true," he agreed solemnly.

Mr. Anderson said, "Stop pulling her leg. Let's let this busy lady get back to work. Besides, she's done a heap of good for this town."

I smiled, sliding some more cinnamon rolls and fruit toward them. Spoiling them was a treat for me as well! These two sweet gentlemen were my favorite customers.

"Ms. Miranda, I just want to hear if you have any prayer requests. You know I am a prayer warrior!" Mr. Oaklan said, looking at me with watery blue eyes.

"Thank you, Mr. Oaklan. A girl can use all the prayers she can get! Will you pray for me as I juggle everything in my life? I need a little more balance."

"I will. Can we pray right now?"

I nodded and held Mr. Oaklan's hands. His long fingers curled around me with a slight amount of pressure. He took a breath, bowed his head, and said, "Father, we need you to help Miranda with everything that is on her plate. Whether she is working or just being a mom to those two great younguns, help her, Lord, in all things. In Jesus' holy name, amen."

"Thanks, Mr. Oaklan."

"He cares, ya know. God really cares about every big or little need you have."

"Thank you for that reminder. Now go enjoy your coffee and cinnamon rolls. I'll come check on you in a bit."

"Sounds good. Sounds good," he said, shuffling his feet toward his favorite table.

A little later in the morning, I came over to the section where many of the senior locals sat, to refill some coffee cups. (Scott and Carrie allowed a free refill of black coffee if you came in.) Mr. Anderson looked at me with his cup out and said, "Say, when are we going to meet this Michael of yours we've heard so much about?"

"Michael will be down tomorrow. Maybe we can stop by on my day off," I said, filling his cup to the brim.

"That would be good. You know he has to measure up to our Mountain Standards...hahaha! Mountain Standard Time... good one!"

The older gentlemen, which also included Mr. Sento, Mr. Ramton, and Mr. Jones belted out laughter.

"True, you guys are some of the best judge of characters I know."

"Well you got characters right!" Mr. Anderson said, elbowing his coffee cronies.

"We won't give him too hard of a time. Seeing that he helped save the town and all from those terrorists," Mr. Oaklan said with respect.

I smiled and said, "Thanks," which went unheard as the discussion was springboarded for the next hour. Including all the details they had heard or read about in the paper regarding the terrorist plots. Also, how the army circumvented a complete attack on the town.

I was amused, chuckling along with the rest as the story grew in exaggerated flair until one of them said, "When Ms. Miranda singlehandedly flew a helicopter over—"

I had to stop the complete hyperbole with an interruption—

"Gentlemen, did you hear the latest about the fishing limit this year?" At this, another heated discussion was launched, and I felt I could safely return to my duty behind the counter. Sometimes, truth was the best avenue to stop rumors.

Michael and I stopped by the following morning. The menfolk were every bit of the class-act I expected. They teased and laughed their way right into his heart. The only serious moment was when they asked Michael about his military background.

"You are on active duty, young man?"

"How long you've been in?"

"Where have you been stationed?"

The questions teemed at him, but when he finished sharing, the nods from the group had respect and maybe a few tears. The knowledge of these men that had been to war bridged the age gap between themselves and Michael. They shook his hand and thanked him for his service. They recognized the cost of freedom more than most.

After that tender and emotional moment, the men broke it up with a few jokes.

"You hear about the kids that never said yes? Well neither did I 'no' anything about it, either."

"Get it, N-O not k-n-o-w!" Mr. Anderson laughed heartily at his own joke as we all chuckled politely. I exchanged amused glances with Michael. He was enjoying himself, and I was relieved. They were characters that peppered any day that was bland.

"Oh, I got one," Mr. Oaklan countered. "What about the fellow who could only walk straight? He didn't have a bend in his step! Get it? He didn't go his own direction."

(I didn't get it, but they did.)

"Hahaha!"

Laughter is contagious, and once you start laughing, it keeps rolling. Pretty soon, the whole corner of the coffee shop contained mirth overarching the rafters in the ceiling. I chuckled just because I enjoyed watching their delighted faces.

Mr. Oaklan rustled his shirt and knocked on the table as the laughter died down. "Did I ever tell you about the time I ran out of wood for the fire? W'all Pa sent me to chop some more, and I moped about, grumbling about the chore. Then Pa comes out, grabs the ax from me, and chops up a good half a cord. I was so impressed that I asked if I could try and chopped at least another fourth of a cord. We hauled that wood back to the woodshed for an hour."

"Was your Ma thankful for the wood?" I wondered aloud.

"Ma was so glad to have some peace and quiet, with me and Pa out there choppin' that she sent my younger brother out there to help as well. We didn't know it, but Ma had paid him a dime to throw the wood back behind the shed. Every time we looked inside the woodshed, it only looked half full. Pa didn't catch on for quite a while. He just kept choppin' and choppin'. Pa finally caught my younger brother chuckin' another armload back behind the woodshed and hauled him up to the front porch. "'Ma,' he called out. 'Does your son, have somethin' to tell me?' Well, Ma started laughin' and laughin'. I can still remember the sound. It was beautiful, like she was. She told us to come inside for a pear cake she had made. Its sweetness always melted in my mouth. They were good, God-fearin' folks, my parents." Mr. Oaklan took a slow bite of his cinnamon roll in tender recollection.

Our time at coffee shop ended on that lighthearted note, and Michael was now officially friends for life with all my coffee regulars.

"Ready to meet my hiking club?" I said as Michael shifted into reverse leaving the parking lot.

"I'm honored to visit with any of your friends. I really enjoyed those fellows back there. Today is already going well, and I've had a great start to my morning. Good coffee and you to share my day with—it can't get much better than that!

"I think you will enjoy the rest of the day with my friends. You already know Giselle and Jerome. I just hope we stay safe," I said, looking serious.

"That's a good thought—safety. Let me pray for everyone right now and for blessings on our day. I promise I'll keep my eyes open, though!" Michael prayed a simple heartfelt prayer, and I was grateful for the lovely day ahead.

Chapter 17

We drove to Indigo Valley trailhead and got out. This particular trip was twofold. We would hike down the trail, which was a strenuous climb, then whitewater raft a little known section of Indigo River. Within our group, we carried four rafts. Each raft could hold up to six people.

It was quite a trek down. The boats weighed around 140 to 150 pounds. The rubber rafts were awkward still with the oars and life jackets tucked inside. The weight of the boats hampered us as we made our way down the steep descent. Based on the knowledge of Thad, one of the hikers and also a river guide for a local company, the river held class IV and V rapids. A friend that owned a school bus would pick us up twenty miles down the river near the old mill.

The "put in" was so far off a convenient roadway that only the locals usually went on this run.

I whispered to Lizzy, "I hope Thad has done his research on how high and fast the river was running," feeling unusually nervous.

Lizzy, never one to keep her thoughts to herself said, "Thad, how's the river, is it safe today?"

"I hit a run yesterday with some friends. It was awesome! The river is high, so the rapids will be intense, but doable," Thad said, enthused.

As we neared the river, we put on life preservers and got in the boats. The river looked placid enough as I eyed the river cautiously. Michael and I sat up at the front. Giselle and Katy were in the middle, and Jerome and Lizzy were in the back. Lizzy reminded us of our coordinated movements and nautical terms: bow, stern, port, starboard, and beam.

"Let's practice a back paddle. We've got to be in sync when we hit the rapids," she said. Lizzy had major expertise. She was on the Colorado River last year as a guide. Quite the outdoorsy type, she had also camped with fellow guides for the whole summer in a tent. She loved it and wanted to do it again next summer. This year, though, she was working through some summer classes studying to become an elementary teacher.

The river curved around rocks and boulders. Occasionally fallen trees tried to snag us, but the fast-paced water surged us forward. Lizzy called the orders as we worked as a team through our first set of rapids. Bouncing down around a boulder, water splashed us in an icy blast.

"Wowzers! That was zany! Good job everybody," Lizzy remarked happily. "Thad said the next rapid is a class V. Be sure to hook your feet under the sides when we ride through it."

The scenery of wild, golden flowers perched on the shores, high banks, heavy forests, and blue skies swept by in a stream of color.

We entered the class V with a whoosh. The boat rocked wildly, and I felt the front of the boat shudder under a wave. Water bulged the front of the boat. I leaned way back, trying to back paddle.

"Michael!" I felt my feet slip out and I tumbled into the cold water. Water rushed over my head. Rocks shoved my body to the left, then the right, like a giant ping-pong game. I tried to keep my body forward with my feet beneath me. The oar was ripped out of my hands, and I lost sight of the boat. I felt a body hit me.

"Giselle!" She had fallen out too, and her head kept going under.

"Hang on, try to keep your body forward." The water separated us, and I slid further down the river. After the rapid, the water continued swiftly. I heard Michael calling my name.

"Miranda, swim over here." Lizzy had steered the boat off to the side. Michael leaned his arms out as I grabbed his hands. He latched onto my drenched life jacket with both hands and tugged me up into the boat.

I sputtered a thanks and said, "I can't see, Giselle!"

"There she is, she's over there!" Jerome shouted. She was in a fast current on the far side of the river. "Her head is up. She's okay—Giselle, try to get to shore," Jerome said frantically.

Giselle waved an arm weakly, but we knew that we would have to launch the raft and adjust our current position.

"Okay, guys—let's hit it!" Lizzy transitioned us back into the flow as we paddled in one accord.

I could see Giselle floundering further to the right. The river pushed her forward.

"We're coming, Giselle, hang on!" Jerome shouted above the white water.

Giselle was propelled forward. A huge boulder with tree limbs pointing viciously at her approached in a matter of seconds. She kicked hard and sidestroked, just missing the jagged tree branches by inches. We all continued to paddle desperately in her direction. Jerome's oars swept the water like a fluid turbine, sending his energy in a forceful path. Their hands reaching, he grabbed her vest as the swift moving current tried to push Giselle under the boat. Jerome then lugged her sopping body up over the edge. Lizzy veered the raft to the shore while Michael swung one of his legs over, letting his foot graze the bottom of an outcrop. I heard the scrape of the gravel under the boat, stopping our speed to a halt. Katy and I gripped the sides of the raft as Michael and Lizzy jumped out and repositioned the bow further on the landing. Jerome got out, cradling Giselle. She looked frail and small in his big arms. He laid her carefully down, checking for injuries. She was absolutely spent.

"Giselle, you okay?" Jerome looked at her tenderly.

"Yes, I think s-so," as she felt a small bruise on her head.

"Did you hit your head hard?" I asked concerned.

"No, I-I'm fine, really. Ju-just give me a m-minute." The water had left her chattering and limp from the exhaustion. A combination of fear and cold had wiped her out. The other boats had gone ahead after we waved them on. The sun began to warm Giselle, slowly bringing the color back to her cheeks.

After about fifteen minutes, Giselle said, seemingly less chilled, "I feel better, let's tackle some more."

The river slowed down to a tranquil rhythm, and we stopped to picnic at a sandy beach. The brave ones jumped from an upper ridge, landing into the deep pool of water. I sat with Giselle who seemed much recovered and enjoyed the sun.

"How are you feeling?" I asked.

"You know, I feel much better now. I'm almost dry and my head doesn't hurt anymore," Giselle replied as she touched her forehead.

"Do you think you should get checked out at the ER?"

"I don't have any signs of a concussion. I'm not dizzy or blurry eyed."

"Well, if you start to feel sick to your stomach or the headache returns, please go today."

"I will. Jerome wouldn't have it any other way. Thanks for caring so much. Your friendship means a lot. Especially since you introduced me to the Lord."

"You and Jerome mean the world to me as well. I thank God for you!" I hugged Giselle.

"Now, what are our guys up too?" I asked as our eyes spotted them in the river.

Michael and Jerome were clowning around the icy water, dunking each other. I got up and waded in. The sun filtered through the leaves, creating a lacy pattern on the river. I looked down and saw some beautiful rocks under my feet. The colors of the river rocks spiraled in onyx, pearly white, and even a touch of coral. Some sparkle remained from a bit of granite co-existing with earth-toned pebbles scattered below the river's surface. I noticed a rock that interested me. Bending down, I let the water flow over my hands as I retrieved it. The weight of the rock was lighter than a pound. It had a watery green color and was shaped like a small footprint. Etched in white streaks was a cross. As I turned the rock over, the exact same shape of the cross was on the other side.

Michael sloshed through the water and asked, "What did you find?"

"Look, it's a cross on a footprint-shaped rock. In fact, it looks like a left footprint with a cross etched on it. As you turn it over, it becomes a right footprint and cross."

"Follow the footprints of Christ!"

"Exactly what I was thinking! I've learned that following Him doesn't mean I always know the end results. Sometimes, I am surprised by what He has planned. Life can be painful, but when you trust God, He can bring about His will."

"That is true. God is always with us, and He helps us through far more than we could ever realize. There have been times in my life when I was crying out to God and He was there, but I didn't know it," Michael said.

"I know and feel the same way. Especially during my divorce, I felt like I was screaming to God and he didn't hear me or care. It was only later that I became aware of His impeccable timing and compassion. You can't rush God, you need to trust God. His presence is there in faith," I said.

"He has been with me in wartime and peace and especially when I found you!" Michael picked me up in his arms and swept me in a circle. My hair flew behind me, cascading outward.

"I love you," Michael said.

"I love you too. God's timing was perfect," I returned with a smile.

After lunch we completed two more rapids with all the fun and thrill I had learned to appreciate. The white water splashed and gurgled with a musical sound as we drifted through the notes.

The river arranged a symphony of crescendos and diminuendos with a few staccato notes for good measure. It had turned out to be a beautiful run down Indigo River. I was hooked and planned to do a river run soon with Ruston and Becca.

Lizzy steered and we landed at the old mill. The ancient bus was waiting, like a steady beacon. Michael and I helped unload the gear and then several of us carried the rafts to the trailer. Once secured, we got on the bus.

I leaned my head on Michael's shoulder and asked, "What did you think of today?"

"I had a great time. I think Ruston and Becca would love it too," Michael said.

"I thought the same thing earlier today. Maybe we can plan a river trip with the local company that Thad works for and have a few of Ruston and Becca's friends come along."

"Isn't Ruston's birthday coming up in a couple of weeks?" Michael said with raised brows.

"June seventeenth," I said.

"Yeah, let's plan a birthday party trip.

"I know Ruston and Becca would have a great time, their friends too."

The weeks flew by as I planned a party for Ruston and managed a busy work schedule. The coffee business was enjoyable as I served many of my regulars. I couldn't help but be involved in people's lives as they filtered in and out of Bean Me Up. Every person had a story, and for the most part, I was interested in the outcome. A reality moment swept in when Mrs. Liddenaul approached the counter. I was prepared for her rude manner, narrow eyes and furrowed brow. However, recently I had begun to engage her in a conversation regarding her pride and joy. Her haughty features softened when I responded with pleasantries, asking about her cat, Penelope.

"She is well, though she doesn't seem herself lately. Maybe she has a cold. I think I will have to take her to the vet, *again*, this week. The vet never seems to do enough for the poor thing. I may have to change vets and drive into Valley Springs. Maybe a doctor with more expertise could handle my kitty's delicate condition."

"Of course, do what you must. I'm sure Penelope will be relieved that you note her sneezes so precisely. Though I don't own a cat, I do believe that cats sneeze sometimes because of their dander and fur. Have you noticed if she has excessive dander?"

"My cat doesn't have dander. I get her bathed at least once a week." At that she was gone, clipping across the room, holding her coffee in her outstretched hand, like a scepter.

"Is she gone?" Katy and Carrie appeared again after having conveniently found busywork in the back while she was here.

"That lady scares me. She once had me remake her coffee three times. After she left, I cried," Katy said.

"She is persnickety about her coffee, that's for sure," Carrie said, agreeing with Katy. "I think it's best if Miranda helps her."

During the next week, Ruston sent a group text out, inviting some of his closest friends to his rafting birthday party and made sure that Becca could invite some too.

Ruston leaned against a wall in the kitchen and said, "I'm stoked! This is going to be sweet!"

Becca was excited too. "Thanks for wanting my friends Abby and Leslie to come along."

"No prob," Ruston said in a mellow voice.

"Honey, you want Gramma and Papa to meet us in the middle for a picnic and cake?" I asked with my phone to my ear.

"Yeah! Can Gramma make her chocolate on chocolate cake, with candy bars on top?" Ruston enthusiastically requested. I flashed back to when he was three years old, staring at me and wondering when it was his birthday so he could eat cake. There is something about a boy and his cake that links his childhood to adulthood, seamlessly.

"Did you hear that, Mom? Ruston wants his favorite cake?" I asked into the phone.

"She said she had already planned to make it!" I said, smiling in Ruston's direction.

"Yep. It's going to be a good birthday!" Ruston said, lacing his fingers behind his head and putting his feet up on the coffee table satisfactorily.

The river raft trip began on a glorious Colorado June morning. We had all the boys in one boat with a guide. Michael, I, Thad, along with Becca, Abby, and Leslie rode in the other. I wasn't surprised that we were all utterly drenched by the first rapid. We rode the river in all its wildness, foam pouring forth in rebounding fashion across the hull of our raft. Dipping low, water would fill to our ankles from the bow to the beam. Our movements mingled with acing the rivers' flow, paddling like mad, and arms surging forward in constant motion through the class III, IV, and V rapids. By the time we arrived at the prearranged lunch spot where Mom and Dad were located, I was only too happy to stop for a rest.

I could still feel the boat moving as an imaginary current swirled around my senses. My arms felt stiff and overworked.

"How is everybody?" Michael asked.

"That was awesome!" the boys and girls said, climbing out of the raft.

"We can't wait to do some more!" one of them shouted.

"Are you hungry?" Mom asked encouragingly.

"Whoo-yeah!" the kids whooped and hollered in agreement.

Dad and Mom had quite a spread. The truck bed was laden with food. Grilled chicken strips, dipping sauces, fresh fruit, various chips, rainbow colors of sports drinks, and of course *the cake*. We all sang "Happy Birthday" as Ruston blew out all eleven sparking candles. He laughed as he and his friends blew them out again once the candles relit themselves. The food was annihilated and the animated talk had ceased slightly to a relaxed frivolity.

I stretched my legs and arms, reaching high. I felt refreshed and ready to complete the rest of the day.

Mom came over and said, "How are you doing, dawlin'?"

"I'm good and thank you. I don't think I could have gone the whole day without y'all refreshing us like you did."

"We were glad to do it. Becca seems to be so happy with her friends dancing over there on that rock slab."

My eyes surveyed the scene of the girls pirouetting and spiraling in semi-graceful form, while Ruston and his friends threw rocks into the river.

"Ruston and Becca are my favorite grandchildren."

"Well, they are your only grandchildren," I said, teasing her.

"True, but that doesn't lessen the joy they bring to us or the love we share with them!" Mom replied with a hug for me.

Dad and Michael were loading the ice chests back in the truck.

"Did y'all get everything?" Mom asked.

"I think so," Dad replied as his eyes swept the area where we picnicked.

"Can one of you boys grab that bag that is blowing away?"

"Ruston and his friends chased after the elusive bag. The bag became filled with air and blew high then low. It was comical as they reached for it only to see it blow further away. Ruston's arm reached out and grabbed it just as it was about to blow into the river. It's the simple things that can bring so much fun.

The second half of the river trip was amazing. Stark cliffs with rugged rock formations stood rigidly against the cerulean cloudless sky. The water was swift as it surged unevenly over bulky rocks. In a dramatic rapid, hues of celadon and emerald poured with the white water as it pummeled over solid boulders.

I was proud at how the boys in the raft ahead paddled rapidly through the waves crashing around them. Their raft was flung forward with a forceful thrust and then launched to the left. You could see their paddles all in the water, dipping low and spurning the water beneath them.

We went next. I felt the raft instantly hit hyperspeed as white water surged us forward into crashing turbulence. We were in the midst of the class V as the raft was jetted down the pike. Cold water splashed in from all sides as we worked our arms in a steady rhythm of stroke, stroke, stroke.

"Back paddle, back paddle on the port. Okay, all stop," Thad commanded.

The girls were wet but ecstatic.

"We loved it!" the girls said.

"I wasn't scared at all," Becca told her friends seated in the center of the raft.

Michael and I had absorbed the most water, like mops in a bucket, since we were up front. We smiled at each other.

"This trip was worth it!" I said.

"With you, anything is worth it!" Michael said winking at me.

Chapter 18

Mrs. Liddenaul made another appearance at the coffee shop the following week. She picked up the conversation about her poor Penelope like we had not stopped talking the other day.

"The vet put Penelope on a diet. Can you believe that? I insisted that she was very healthy and ate a variety of omega-3s in her diet. I personally cooked all her fish according to her liking. The veterinarian said that Penelope was so large that she couldn't properly groom herself and the dander was a sign that she needed to slim down. Of all the nerve! My poor, poor Penelope. What will she do?" She muffled a sob.

"Now, now, Mrs. Liddenaul. I'm sure the vet has Penelope's best interest in mind. Keep her on the special diet, and soon, big...uh, I mean little Penelope will return to a healthy weight."

I tried to keep my voice soothing for her frayed nerves. I knew that Mrs. Liddenaul had very few friends. This really was a social call for her, and I did my best to treat her like I would any friend.

"You know you're the only one around here who gets my coffee right...Miranda."

I knew that she had just given me a compliment.

"I'm happy to do it for you. Now, would you like to try our new warm carrot cake muffins with a cream cheese drizzle?"

"Absolutely not, I'm on a diet." She whirled around, almost spilling her coffee, and left. I saw her look back for a moment and knew that she was curious about my expression.

I waved slightly, and she nodded regally in my direction. This friendship would take some work, but I knew God was opening a door for me to show His love to a very lonely woman.

After work, I picked up the children from school and then went straight home. I ran upstairs to take a quick shower before starting supper. I let the hot water pulse over my skin as I considered the day's events. Ruston had practiced with his coach in the afternoon, so his uniform needed washing. Becca would be going to dance Thursday and would have to have her leotard and ballet slippers returned to her dance bag. Supper tonight would be waffles and some sausage links. It was easy.

As I toweled off, I heard a scream from downstairs. Leaping down the steps, with my towel drawn about me, I called out, "What's the matter? What happened? Is everybody okay?"

Becca came running over sobbing, "Ruston took my controller. I had it first!"

"It was my turn. She always takes the one that works. But she's the one that broke the button on the other one," Ruston said, yanking on the gaming device that was in his hand.

"Okay. First of all, I thought somebody was hurt. Becca don't scream like that unless it's an emergency. Ruston, you need to share and wait your turn. Don't take something out of your sister's hand. That's how things break. We can't afford to buy another one. Okay?"

"Yes, ma'am," Becca replied tearfully.

"Yes, ma'am," Ruston said glumly.

"Guys, I love you, and we need to work together as a family. Life is too precious to fight over a silly game. Now, let me get dressed, y'all need to apologize, and then we'll make some delicious waffles!"

"Yeah, that sounds so good! You're right, Mom, we need to help you by getting along," Ruston said, hugging his sister.

"Thanks you guys. I know that you can do it!"

I smiled, shaking my head as I went upstairs to throw on an oversized T-shirt and some tattered workout pants. I wanted to be comfortable while I made supper.

"Mom, these waffles are amazing!" Ruston said as he bit into his fourth waffle.

"Can I have another sausage?" Becca asked sweetly.

"Sure, honey."

I may not be the best cook in the world, but I love my kids and they loved me. That had to count for something!

August arrived and with it a new school year for the children. After school that next week Ruston looked kind of down.

"Ruston, is something wrong?"

"Coach says I need to work on my start. He says I'm dragging. Can we work on it today?"

"Of course, let's set up cones on the sidewalk out front and then I'll time you."

"Okay, thanks!" Ruston said as he brought Bowie and Maui to the front yard and secured their leashes.

Becca helped me set up the cones while I set my phone to timer.

"Almost got it. Okay, yeah it's ready. Ruston, are you ready?"

Ruston knelt down on the sidewalk, his hands pressed on the ground and his feet ready to spring him forward.

"On your mark, get set, go!" I said as Ruston lunged forward and sprinted to the farthest cone.

"Three seconds. Let's try again and get it to one second."

"Sure."

Ruston sprinted off after the word "go," and the timer on my phone read two and a half seconds.

"Try again," I said, pushing Ruston to not give up.

"Okay."

After resetting the clock and running the short course about six times, Ruston said, "Mom, I'm no good."

"Hey, you're getting better. Keep it up! One more time. On your mark, get set—go!"

Ruston rocketed forward, and the readout on my clock said one second as he passed the final cone.

"You did it! See, you kept trying and you improved. I'm proud of you and so is God!"

Ruston hugged me as Becca danced up and down in a cheerleading outfit, waving yellow pom-poms that she had managed to throw on during the practice.

"Go Ruston! G-O spells GO! Yay!" Becca shouted out enthusiastically. She proceeded to exhibit a lopsided cartwheel. The dogs tapped their tails in applause.

"Thanks, Becca. You make a great cheerleader. You'll have to wear that to my next game. I think it helped!" Ruston said, winking at her.

"I can do that!" Becca said as her eyes sparkled at the thought.

God helped me that day to coach my son. He gave me the ability to teach Ruston what a dad usually did. I'm far from a perfect parent, but I was present in my child's life when he needed me. I'm grateful as a single mom that I was never alone as a parent. God was the ultimate "present Father." He was the Abba-Daddy that never quit. He provided the wisdom and stamina I needed every day to be the creative, loving, and persevering mom I needed to be in order to raise my children in the ways of God. *Thank you, God!*

Chapter 19

My hiking group had settled on Rembrandt Trail. I think it was named that for the beauty it inspired. Artists would usually haul easels to a spot on a butte one mile from here. The panoramic vista was beyond breathtaking. Rivers became tiny threads of blue expertly sewed into a tan and gray quilt. Houses miles away, stacked precariously against a mountain, clung to their plot of dirt beneath its surface. Each home was someone's dream, snubbing its nose to the dangers of winter ice and clinging to the promise and beauty of the springtime.

Hiking along the route, our hiking club, along with Katy, her friend Rock, Lizzy and I saw the green markings painted on tall aspen trees. "This way," the trees seemed to say, proudly bearing their small swatch of paint along the trail. We followed the trail to the river. Rocks placed within a few feet of each other created a shaky bridge across a rushing mountain stream.

I felt a light shower sprinkle down on me. It was refreshing after the arduous path. However, the soft rain turned into a downpour as we steadily ascended on the trail. I felt my hair weigh down as wet tendrils began to send droplets into my eyes with every step. My boots splooshed in the mud, and I fell to my knees, coating my hands in sticky black mud as I caught myself. I adjusted my backpack and searched for a walking stick to steady my gait.

Katy saw me and stopped.

"You go ahead—I'll be right behind you," I said, my head down, searching the underbrush. I backtracked back down the trail, finally spotting a long, reliable, walking stick. I leaned on it, testing its strength. Perfect! I stood still for a moment, listening to the quietness of the steady rain. A bird twittered, singing about the day—a twig cracked as it broke.

I heard a distant accented voice behind me, "Miranda Colvin. Turn around, we know who you are." I fell forward in sheer terror. A bullet, a fraction above me, whizzed over my head.

Ice and heat went down my chilled body, and I stopped breathing. I began to run, slipping uphill. I didn't recognize the voice, but I knew the cold words could only mean one thing— they found me again.

I planted my stick into the ground, hearing the squelch as it sank down. The stick became a wobbly javelin, launching me over the steep trail, catapulting me over stumpy roots and slippery moss. My senses heightened, my eyes alert for the group in front of me. Where are they? I leapt up the trail, ever mindful of the deep panic in my chest and the heavy footsteps behind me as they slipped up the steep trail. Occasionally, a bullet zinged ahead of them, stubbing the bark of a tree next to me. As the path leveled, I took off in a runner's all-out stride. My arms pumping like pistons.

My dad's words came to my mind, "Breathe two in, one out, lengthen your stride, stretch your legs all the way from your hips, and let your arms propel your forward."

Ahead of me I could see some markings. One tree had one dash, the other held two. I prayed the group had turned to the right by the two dashes. The rain was heavy, a complete downpour. The trees above me shrouded the sun, creating a canopy of darkness almost like an eerie nightglow. I plunged deeper into the shadowy woods, losing sight of the trail for a moment. I began to breathe laboriously, maintaining a fast stride. I was growing weary at this pace, when some thick brambles tripped me, causing me to stumble. The forest closed in further as low branches caught my hair, ripping out a few strands. I began to pray, *Lord, hide me, cover me.*

My breathing grew steady again, and I felt a burst of speed come over me, working my legs, before my brain could send them the message. I continued, locating the trail again. Beneath the broken covering of the tree limbs, the rain washed my footsteps into a river where the trail had once been. I longed for rest and then I saw some huge rocks ahead. The ivy growing over the rocks hung over the edge. Maybe, I could hide behind it. My mind challenged me that they would see me, but I felt a glimmer of hope eyeing the cleft of the rock. I changed course, leapt over the trail, and plunged into the forest. I slid my body behind the ivy, my back against the rock.

Minutes later, I heard footsteps quickly marching purposefully down the path, the air around me closed in, feeling inky and sinister. My blood pumped in my ears, reverberating the rhythm almost audibly. The men paused and then passed menacingly by in slow, deliberate stomps. I stayed in my hiding place, breathing with a shallow breath. The rain dripped through the leaves, plastering my already wet skin in another coat of liquid. My muddy knees were tightly woven into my chest. I wanted to stretch them, but fear trapped me—alone. I refused to allow the fear to overwhelm me, *God I know you are with me. Show me the path that I should go, for to you I lift up my soul.* Verse after verse flooded my soul:

> Let the morning bring me word of your unfailing love, for I have put my trust in you. Show me the way I should go, for to you I entrust my life.
>
> —Psalm 143:8

> Trust in the LORD with all your heart and lean not on your own understanding; in all your ways submit to him, and he will make your paths straight.
>
> —Proverbs 3:5–6

The footsteps I so dreaded to hear came back. Loud, furtive strikes on the ground, each muddy step sucking the boot, prematurely delaying the next step. Finally both sets of boots stopped right in front of me, as if waiting for me to make the next move. *This is it, I'm tired of this deadly game.* I fingered the strands of my ivy fortress and stepped out into the open.

"Miranda?"

"Katy, Rock, Lizzy?" my voice shook with relief.

"We've been searching for you! I finally just prayed with Rock and Katy and asked God for help. What are you doing in there, playing hide-and-seek?" Lizzy queried.

I replied with a question of my own. "Did some men pass you on the trail?"

"Now, that you mention it, two guys startled our group a few minutes ago as they looked us slowly over," Katy said.

"Look, those guys are dangerous. Did they follow you?"

Rock looked serious as he spoke slowly, "No, I think they thinned out ahead of us."

"Did the rest of the group stay together?" I asked pensively.

"Some of the group were already ahead. We broke apart from the group we were with to come back for you," Rock informed me.

"I told them we would see them later. I couldn't imagine why you were taking so long. You think the men are from the same terrorist organization that tried to hurt you before?" Lizzy said, her hand on her mouth.

"I believe they are. They knew my name. It must have been leaked to them from one of the reports or maybe the local newspaper article," I speculated. "I don't know how they found out about me, but they did and this is happening. We can't go back in case they are waiting for us at the parking lot. We need to move now, and maybe Lizzy can check the trail map. There must be another way up the mountain."

"We should head to a ranger station," Rock said.

"Exactly. We need to travel fast. Lighten your backpacks, or just leave them here," I said.

Rock stashed the backpacks behind a rock and we set off in the opposite direction of the way out.

The rain lightened.

"I'm sorry that you are involved. I thought this was behind me."

"We're in this together. We're ford the river at the lower falls and head north to Timberline Trail," Lizzy said, perusing the trail map.

We began the trek through the thick foliage. My fear antenna was raised. Every branch that broke after the rain, as it slipped to the forest with a thud, caused me to jump unconsciously. We were moving fast through the forest, not speaking, breathing hard with the adrenaline. The trail was so wet that we stayed above the trail, scurrying through the woods. As the trail twisted, we would hop down to the lower level of tree roots or rocks. We got to the stream-turned-river, but it seemed impassable. The rain had sent a fierce anger over the water, thrashing rocks and tree limbs in its path.

"We'll hike the rushing river along the banks. At some point it will narrow, and we can cross," I said, breathing hard. Negative thoughts hampered my normally optimistic nature as we tromped through the vegetation that lingered near the rushing water. I can't believe this is happening again. I will be amazed if we can outrun them, I know they can outgun us, considering that I don't have even one. There was a time when I couldn't care less about guns. Now I wish I had one of Michael's semiautomatic, fully loaded M-9s right about now.

"Look, if something happens to me, I want you to run. Do not stop to help me. This is not your war," I commanded them.

"Sorry, Miranda, but this is your friends that you are talking to. God is going to help us through this," Lizzy said, trying to erase my martyr-style phrases.

"I think I can speak for all of us when I say, we are with you until the end, whatever that may be," Rock said as Lizzy and Katy murmured in agreement.

"Okay, I…thanks." I was silent for a moment, lost in my thoughts. I was no longer alone. Not only was God with me, but He had sent me encouragement in the form of friendship.

"Up ahead, what do you think, will it work?" Katy said, pointing to an old tree that had been struck by lightning and had fallen across the now raging stream.

I could see that the tree was old and mostly rotten as the water had been absorbed into its bark. The final steps across would be challenging because we had to climb over the huge, heavy branches that clung to the dirt and rocks on the opposite bank. Rock, Katy, Lizzy, and I began to pick our way across, one at a time. Rock went first, testing for strength in each step.

"I think it's holding—" As he was speaking, bark broke off and his right leg slipped, dangling it below the tree into the water. The rushing water tugged, pulling him to his stomach. He crawled back up onto his elbows and said with a grin, "Watch that weak spot in the wood. It's like Australia—it might take you down under."

Katy giggled at his classic clownism.

Slowly he proceeded to cover the rest of the way, knees bent in almost a squat, as he maintained balance. At the branches, he picked a large, low one that reached to the shore and stood on it while gripping the upper branches. When he reached the other side, we all breathed a sigh of relief.

Katy and Lizzy went next. Leaning on a branch for support, Katy lost her balance as the twig snapped, apparently water-rotted. She righted herself with a quick two-step of her feet. Lizzy had reached the heavy branches, and Rock stretched a hand to help her across. Katy followed, but as the weight shifted, the tree rolled slightly, the upper branches falling into the river. She shuffled her feet, but she still fell down sideways, her left elbow scraping on the wood. She righted herself and crawled the rest of the way on all fours. Rock and Lizzy held out their hands over the now large gap of the tree limbs and bank. She held their hands, regripping twice in hesitation, then was swung the rest of the way. I could see the tree had now changed positions. The current was beginning to take control of the tree. The limbs groaning in protest, I watched in horror as it plunged below the current. Three quarters of the tree was now submerged, a few roots held it to my side of the shore.

I stood there for a moment, surveying the surrounding area. Was there another tree I could climb across? Maybe further downriver, I could glimpse some rocks. My pondering was disrupted by a deluge of remotely located gun chatter.

Instantaneously, I heard a triumphant shout of "We've got her stranded!"

I leapt onto the rotten tree and scrambled low, water seeping up along the tree branches. Rock, Katy, and Lizzy had laid down on the ground, reaching for me. I pointed my index and middle finger together, like an airline stewardess, indicating the "emergency exit doors" were downriver. Lizzy understood with an affirmative nod and crawled to some underbrush. Rock and Katy followed, stooping low, as gun fire sprang into life again, denting trees and spurning dirt. I felt bullets graze my leg and arm; the pain pierced me, immobilizing my calf and left bicep. I dove forward, rapidly dragging my leg and then buried my body into the heavy branches, which were now mostly underwater, hoping that the limited covering would protect me for a moment. I looked for the first time in their direction and saw a heavyset man and thin-as-paper companion, both in black with artillery strapped across their chests.

"*Baradarm!*" I heard the Arabic word, which translates as "my brother" echo up the mountain. "I will avenge my brother!" The thin one screamed at me again, his fist pulsated the air. His black eyes and tan skin looked pale under the sunless sky, like he was malnourished. It was probably drugs and hate that made him appear so insanely ruthless. Apparently, this foe was a blood-relation to one of the terrorists that had been killed or captured. I was probably on a long list of names of people they were pursuing for vengeance. The thick-stomached terrorist next to him grabbed his gun and shot, aiming expertly at my haven of branches. I wriggled my body back into the icy waters, fighting the branches, then shoved my body, feet first, into the icy current. The snow-melted water zinged my body, giving me an immediate headache. (The good news was that I no longer felt my injured leg and arm. Or maybe that was the bad news.) Either way, the numbing current had a mind of its own. I couldn't hear if the bullets were hitting the water over the rushing gurgle surrounding me, but I knew they were aiming straight for my head. I continued to hold my breath and prayed I could float further downstream.

A rock hit my outstretched foot, sending me sideways. I felt my face bounce up toward the surface. I breathed in the crisp air, reviving my dull senses. The bullets pattered the water next to my right hand, I pulled it to me like I had been burned. I was back under now, floating downstream like a branch, whirling around one rock and then the next. I came up for air and tried to look closely at the left bank. I couldn't see anything but trees and rocks. I prayed, *God please protect me.* A huge surge swept me around, my head now facing downriver, then the current pulled my arms backward, followed by my back, then my feet kicked over the edge, like a gymnast doing a back handspring.

I felt my body falling.

The weight of the falls anchored me deep below the crashing aftermath. At the base of the falls, a deep pool had gathered. It was complete darkness as I touched bottom, having somersaulted several times until I was right side up. I weakly sprang back up to the surface, suffocating from a lack of oxygen. The water spun me over to a dark area of green deep water close to a rocky ledge. I breathed in huge lungfuls of air as if I'd never tasted it before.

I reached out to grasp the rock wall to slow my pace, but my fingers and short nails dragged only the slick rocks, which were coated in moss and algae. The deep waters flow buffered me for the moment from any jagged rocks as I floated. I breathed deeply and saw a lower rock landing ahead, perhaps four feet off the water. A tree branch, thick with foliage was in my view, and I aimed my body straight into it.

Unsure if I could even pull myself out of the water, I clung there for a moment, grasping a branch in each hand, feeling the steady current rift with white water scuttling over my neck and shoulders. I took one more breath, praying as I did for strength, and reached for another branch, one hand over the other, not letting go of the branch until the other hand was on a secure limb. My shoes touched the slick rock edge of the outcrop, and I pulled again at the branches, planting myself on the rock below the water's surface. I high kicked my leg onto more branches, until I was straddling the tree and the rock ledge. Reaching for something to propel my body onto the ledge, I heard the underbrush ahead of me shake and move backward.

Chapter 20

I blinked, ready to throw myself back into the water when my eyes focused on Lizzy and Rock emerging from the forest. They pulled me onto the tree lined rocky outcrop, and I rested for a moment. The heavy tree in front of me hid us slightly

"Where's Katy?"

"I'm here, I'm okay...ow," Katy came, stumbling over with a blood stained T-shirt tied around her left arm.

"We tried to watch you as we ran," Katy said.

"You were under the water completely. I never saw you breathe. I thought maybe the bullets had taken you..." Lizzy said, looking concerned as her eyes misted with tears.

"We couldn't see you most of the time until you went over the ten-foot waterfall," Rock noted heavily, like he was still in shock.

"I went over the falls?" I asked incredulously before the memory of tumbling helplessly through whitewater surged through my mind. "Oh, that must have been when—" I shuddered and took a deep breath for good measure.

"Does it hurt?" Lizzy asked, peering at me. Her eyes strayed to the streaks of blood on my arm and calf. "Here, let me take a look at that," she said, reaching for me.

Perhaps the panic of almost drowning had caused me to momentarily ignore my injuries, but Lizzy's attention to them now brought back the pain in searing waves.

We moved further back into the woods as Rock ripped the bottom half of his flannel shirt to wrap around my arm and leg. Lizzy secured it tightly with several knots; I felt pain, but also relief. I was glad to see my friends. We had to get to the ranger station before the terrorists found a way across the raging rapids. With so much water pumping down the overflowing rapids, it would take hours for them to hike around them.

"What are we going to do?" Katy wailed loudly.

"Shh. We need to keep quiet and not expose our position," I said firmly.

I felt compassion for her, but I knew the level of danger was increased every moment we stood still talking about our problematic situation.

"Rock, put your arm around Katy and let's get ahead of these guys," I commanded.

My earlier instincts were in high gear. I felt the prickle of fear on my skin but washed it down with a surge of adrenaline.

"We head out now, behind the trees lining the water, north to Timberline trails. A strenuous, steep climb is ahead and we will need every ounce of strength we have in reserve," Lizzy said.

"Look, everyone, I'm sorry about this," I said, lifting my injured leg up over a rock.

Katy spoke first. "Don't think about it. We want to help you. I'm sorry I lost it earlier."

"Hey, we are all entitled to our freak-out moments," I said, giving Katy a smile in understanding.

"Those are the times when we cry out to God. He will use this time of suffering and fear for our benefit, if we let him," Lizzy said.

Rock turned to me and said, "We are going to make it. Let's just stick together."

His confidence brought solidarity to our group. I was glad he was along.

"God be with us as we seek to find peace in the storm. Help us to quickly locate the ranger station and please provide protection for us as we hike there," I prayed aloud quietly.

"Amen," my friends replied in unison.

The wet, muddy hike was exhausting. Wet leaves and branches released the rain on our faces, scorning its droplets. Brambles and vines caught our ankles, and we slipped up the muddy incline, only to slide down the next embankment. Cutting straight up the mountain instead of taking switchbacks, our muscles trembled with the undue strain. When I heard Rock say something a little too loudly to Katy, I stressed our need for silence with my index finger raised to my lip. I was paranoid that any sound we made would alert our pursuers to our location. A great darkness seemed to settle on the northern edge of the mountain. More than just the dark clouds that hovered and rolled in the sky, I felt the spiritual oppression that comes when an attack is near.

"A couple more miles, and we should be seeing the station," Lizzy said softly, pulling out her map from her pocket. "We need to transverse this upper portion of Timberline Trail, pass the cave near Springs River, then follow the ridge to the ranger station."

"The cave, mmm," Rock murmured. "That is not well known."

"I only know about it because we hiked that trail last year," Lizzy said.

"I went to the cave too. I remember Mitch brought his giant flashlight and after going in with the group, he turned it off for a few minutes. That darkness was so inky that I literally couldn't see my hand in front of me," Katy said.

"Well, we have a hiding place in plan if things get hot," I said, muffling my voice.

In the distance I heard a helicopter. The chopping blades whirred like thunder. Lightning cracked the sky.

"Hey, we're saved!" Katy said, elated.

Hiking to an open rock that exposed us to the wind, we waved our arms wildly. The helicopter swept in, bending the trees in its wake. I felt a moment of deep panic as my eyes registered who the pilot was.

"It's the terrorist's brother. Get down—run!" I screamed.

Bullets rained down from automatic artillery mounted to the front of the chopper. Our arms gripped our heads as our bodies lowered in a hunched run. We ran until the trees blocked their view of us.

Rock said, "To the cave!"

We sped off in an all-out, bell-lap-now-or-never run. Our fears were inundated by the sound of the helicopter beating the air behind us as we clamored for a safer location. We ran hard, covering a huge amount of ground, ducking low beneath the trees for cover.

"The cave is this way." Rock leapt ahead of me, dodging bullets that spiked through the leaves.

We reached the edge of some gigantic boulders, which seemed so heavy that the mountains were weighted and anchored by its rocky substance.

"Stay back, we're here," Rock instructed. "The helicopter will make a sweep for us, as they pass, we will stay out of sight. Afterward, we will go in."

We nodded, hiding low under some branches.

The helicopter swung low over our heads, seeming to hover like it had spotted us. I closed my eyes, expecting the worse. The wind tore at the leaves above us; they quivered violently, resembling my body as it shook with a spasm of fear. In a moment, the flying metal bird was gone, leaving dust swirling around our faces.

Rock nodded, and we ran to the rocks.

I didn't see anything until Lizzy and Rock pulled back a large, desolate bush that covered the black void. Katy and I stepped up first, as Lizzy and Rock restrained the bush. Lizzy and Rock scampered in, and Rock released the limbs of the branches back over the opening, blocking the sunlight. Through the dim light, I could see that ancient white and gray rock walls surrounded us in a narrow tunnel. I heard the slow drip of water from somewhere deeper in the cave.

"We need to move to the main room of the cave. There is pure water to drink, and we can spread out better to rest," Rock said.

It was dark then went darker still as we crept, holding hands to the cave's main cavernous space. We inched along, bumping our head occasionally on the low ceiling. Soon, cool air swept in our direction. I could somehow sense the ceiling height grow higher. We must have reached the large space they had talked about. The sound of a trickling waterfall dripped into a large pool.

"Are you sure the water is safe to drink?" I asked thirstily.

"Speleothems such as stalagmites and stalactites border the drip pools. Water contained in the calcium carbonate rocks have percolated through and now the water is pretty much filtered," Katy said knowledgeably.

Our shock at her scientific knowledge was profound as we were rendered speechless.

"What? One of my courses in science at the college went over this a few weeks ago."

"Katy, I'm impressed!" Rock said.

We all leaned over the edge and scooped some water into our parched mouths. The sweet, cold water sated my tongue. I dripped the water on my head, cooling my hot skin. The last couple of miles we had run were a feat beyond athletic. I breathed in and took another sip.

"Wish I could bottle this!" Rock said, drinking the water again.

"It's like none I've ever tasted," Lizzy pronounced.

"Would you like some more?" Katy said, splashing the water in Lizzy's direction.

"No, but maybe you would," Lizzy said with a swipe from the pool.

We all needed a moment to loosen our minds from the sheer terror we had experienced a half an hour before. I didn't begrudge them that. My thoughts turned inward.

These men had resources. A helicopter was just one asset a large connected terrorist group would have at their disposal. I couldn't even wrap my mind around the fact that an hour ago, my opponents were standing on the embankment. How did they get a helicopter up here so fast? Apparently, they had planned ahead for a quick getaway before they had begun the hike. This elaborate scheme of killing me and wreaking destruction was my undoing. I felt my legs collapse and fell into a heap. Maybe this was a terrible dream that I was in.

"Wake me, Lizzy, from this nightmare." I pounded the cold ground and vaguely looked in her direction through my tears.

"Girl, this is real. I'm in it too," she reassured me.

Rock leaned over and took my hand. "God is bigger than this situation. The Bible says, 'Nothing is impossible with God.'"

Katy hugged me, her warmth stealing away the bit of sadness and dread that had seemingly overcame me.

"Do we stay here or move on?" Rock voiced my thoughts.

"Where does the cave go?" I asked.

"I'm not sure. It narrows, I know that. We turned around last time we came," Lizzy said.

"If we try, we might have a better chance of escape than if we went back the way we came in," I said pointedly. We were in dire straits. I needn't tell them of our limited chances of surviving this ordeal. If we were to continue back to the entrance, the mountain fell away. The towering trees became bushes, and there would be nothing to hide under.

"I think we should at least try to go further into the cave," Rock said.

"Katy, Lizzy?" I asked.

"We're in," their voices answered in unison.

"God be with us," I prayed aloud.

The cave narrowed at the edge of the room back to tunnel form. We hunched down and walked, hands outstretched, unable to see what we would find next. A rock wall? A wild animal? We began to crawl as the cave's ceiling narrowed. My heart pounded with theirs as we made our way down a deep passageway. How the cave could grow darker, I do not know, but it did. Unseeing, my eyes could not adjust to the deep darkness. Black, red, and green spots would roll across my eyes as I blinked again and again, searching for light. A cool wet wind swept in through the cave, moistening our faces. I heard distant thunder rumbling as it resounded on the cave's ribs.

"Did you hear that?" Katy asked fearfully.

"What a racket!" Rock said.

"Maybe this is a good thing," I said in wonderment. "If I can hear thunder, maybe we are nearing something beyond the cave."

"A way out?" Lizzy said with hope tingeing her voice.

The cave seemed to morph into a shadowy, grayish blue light. The walls opened up from their claustrophobic status to a narrow roomlike space. We were in close quarters as we squeezed to the center, our arms touching each other and the sides of the walls as the cave became wide enough for us to stand upright. Our crouched form stretched to full length, my muscles taut, aching with the strain from the past infant position.

"A hole!" Katy said, pointing above our heads to a full-moon–shaped opening.

"It looks big enough, but how do we reach it?" Rock said, inspecting the narrow opening, at least twelve or fourteen feet high. Lizzy laced her fingers together, boosting Katy, who was the lightest, up first. She used the sides of the wall to balance her precarious position until she grabbed a thick tree root near the opening. Swinging a foot onto the side of the wall, she pulled herself through. Disappearing for a moment, Katy popped her head back in, lowering a vine she had unwound from a tree. I offered for Lizzy to go next, but she insisted I go first.

"Thanks!" I grasped the vine and inched up, using my knees to lock in my progress. The side walls of the cave loomed closer, and I kicked my feet over to the wall and used it to "walk" further up to the top.

"Bring me a souvenir from your trip up!" Lizzy called as a rock pelted down from the top.

"That was fast," Lizzy said, shielding her head.

"Sorry about that. Somebody should do something about the loose terrain," I said facetiously. I thanked God for this heaven-sent opening as I was pulled myself through. Katy gripped the vine as she accelerated my ascent back to civilization, or at least, earth. Katy and I hugged in relief.

"Lizzy's next," I said, helping Katy tug on the vine.

Lizzy came up, her smile reaching us before she did.

"Girls, we made it!" we said as we hugged.

"Hey, a little help down here!" Rock had his hands on his hips, looking at us through the hole in the sky.

We threw the vine back down, as all three of us lugged and pulled with all our might. We heaved further still, and Rock seemed suspended for a moment. The vine splintered and began to stretch to a thin thread.

"Quick, it's breaking."

We leaned back, yanking with one final lunge to the vine, out sprawled Rock onto the rocky edge.

We all high-fived as we realized that we had made it out—alive!

I turned around looking through the trees and glimpsed a raised structure about a mile away.

"Look, the fire tower. Rangers usually transmit information about possible forest fires here. They will have a radio."

"What if no one's there? I've heard that sometimes, there are too many areas for a ranger to cover," Katy said.

"This is one time when breaking and entering will probably be allowed," I said.

We ran through the forest, sneaking under open areas exposed to the sky, one at a time. I didn't hear any sounds of the helicopter. We just needed to get into the tower, transmit our coordinates, and get rescued. I felt weary as we trod the earth. Trees thinned as boulders and rocks were under our feet, leaving only bits of dirt where a scrub brush persevered. A sheer drop-off was on our left, and I could see another tree line ahead of us.

I noticed the mountain rock ledge we were running on had a deep crack in it. The layers of the thin, weather-beaten rock appeared fragile as brittle pieces of rock scuffed under my hiking boots. I heard, before I felt, a loud, cracking sound under our feet.

"What was that?" Lizzy said.

"Run!" Rock yelled.

We sped inward, but still to the north toward the trees in a diagonal path. Lizzy and I were together with Rock and Katy ahead of us in the distance. The huge rock slab we were running across trembled then began to slide down, breaking away from its tenuous links to the mountain. Our feet tilted underneath us. I felt a rushing wind, then my feet felt air. I was leaping in the air, over to the tree line. I knew that at that moment, I was going to fall to my death.

Chapter 21

The air electrified around us as the wind whipped my clothes. Plunging, I felt a peace steal over me, cushioning my body until I felt light warm my body. Instantaneously, Lizzy and I landed onto the leaf-strewn dirt. We were on the ground where Katy and Rocky stood.

I looked at Lizzy incredulously and said, "Did that just happen?"

"I know it was God that saved us. He sent an angel to hoist us up."

"It had to have been. I was falling," I said, amazed.

"Me too. The rock seemed to have splintered away into— nothing," Lizzy said, dumbfounded.

"I've always read that verse, 'He will give His angels charge over you.' Now I know what that means," I said.

"You could have died. I saw you begin to go down," Katy said, confounded by what she had just witnessed.

"But we didn't," I said, clear-eyed. I had just experienced a miracle. My own miracle. God was as real as he was in the Old Testament and the New. God was present and alive, and He had a plan for our lives. I felt overjoyed as God's love enveloped my heart. A renewed vigor set in, and we ran for the ranger's look-out station.

We were near the summit when I reached the first metal stair step and started climbing. It looked to be about fifty feet up. This view shed had a metal cab that had been built in what looked to be the 1960s. Though it was vintage, many forest rangers believed it was still necessary to have a human pair of eyes scoping the landscape for the chance of fire. This was the kind of lookout that had a metal "cab" at the top. I could see below me that my friends were following me up the steps. I felt dizzy at the approximate five stories I was climbing up. I swayed slightly then tightened my sweaty palms on the metal handrail. Upon reaching the top landing, I breathed deeply, clutching the spindly railing, seeing the 360-degree panorama around me. Grabbing the doorknob, I felt it turn slightly then click to a set lock. I peered into the windows seeing a one-room shelter with a table, containing a radio and a bed. There was no one in there.

I cried in defeat. "There is no one here. What if this thing isn't even operational?"

Rock looked up, giving me a thumbs-up. "We will break in like you said and deal with it. At least we will have a better vantage point."

I nodded, but before I could turn around, the door swung open behind me. Hearing a click, I swallowed hard and turned to face a gun cocked and ready to shoot. But the person holding the gun instantly took the forefront of my attention.

"Michael?"

"Miranda! What are you doing here?" he asked, slowly reholstering his gun.

"I didn't see you." I was still so surprised, I didn't register his question.

"I was standing behind the door because I wasn't expecting any visitors. I was trying to get a visual of the terrorists, and then I heard voices."

Rock, Katy, and Lizzy appeared at the railing. Their eyes were open wide. Lizzy hugged Michael. Then Rock and Katy came forward. Rock shook hands with Michael as Katy gave him a big squeeze. Michael stepped back into the house, allowing us more room to stand.

"This is unbelievable! You're here!" I said in a relieved voice.

"Expecting someone else?" Michael teased.

I hugged Michael, gave him a kiss, and held his hands. "No, I…we had hopes for someone to help us. God knew exactly what I needed."

"Miranda, you said *help us.* What in the world is going on? You shouldn't be here. This area is an active combat zone."

"Michael, they found me. They tried to kill me. While they were shooting, I had to go over a waterfall, practically drowned myself in the process, run through the forest at a breakneck speed, hide in a cave to escape a helicopter with artillery guns…"

Michael interrupted me, with a kiss. After a moment, he held my face and said, "Thank God you're okay. My love—what would I do without you?"

"True. That's a good question. Now what can we do to find relief from all this madness?"

"I've got men spread out in the forest. I'm surprised you didn't run into anyone. We got word through a code breakthrough about a terrorist presence and set up a base camp at the main lodge. I was working aerial. Especially after we learned of an unauthorized helicopter flying over the forest."

"Do you know if there is a first-aid kit up here?" Lizzy interjected, peering around the room.

"Over here, in the cabinet by the bed."

Lizzy opened a white metal box that contained ointment, gauze, packets of OTC meds, adhesive bandages, and surgical tape. "Katy, you first."

Katy sat down on the edge of the bed while Lizzy stripped off the old T-shirt clinging to her arm. "Do you have any water up here?"

"No running water, but here are a few water bottles I brought up with me," Michael said as he unzipped his heavy canvas duffel bag and threw one to Lizzy.

Lizzy spilled the water over the wound, washing away any dried blood. Next, she covered the area heavily with ointment overlaid with gauze and secured with strips of medical tape.

"You're next, Miranda."

Lizzy applied the same diligence in cleansing and binding my wounds.

"Miranda, I can't believe they got to you. I am so sorry that they hurt you. I wish…I could have been there to protect you," Michael said, wincing while I held back a few unshed tears of pain.

"God was with me—us. I know that He kept us safe. We are alive because God deemed it to be so. Our greater purpose has been fulfilled because of the perseverance of this day. God has used this experience to draw me closer to Him and to recognize that not only is He present in every circumstance, but that He provided a way out."

"Tell Michael about your miracle!" Katy said, slightly awed.

"God did a miracle today. He saved Lizzy and I from 'rock bottom.' I want you to know I literally lived the verses in Psalm 91:11–12, 'For He will command His angels concerning you, to guard you in all your ways. They will lift you up in their hands, so that you will not strike your foot against a stone.' A rock shelf broke away from the mountain while we were on it. I can't explain it fully, but one minute I was falling to my death, then a light storm that was both fierce and powerful swept over my body, and Katy's too, back up the mountain and we landed safely on solid ground."

"You are a survivor...you all are, that's for sure. I am over-whelmed at the mercy of God for bringing you through. This situation with the terrorists is a face-off. We are going to end this nightmare—today."

We filled Michael in on some of the terrorists' last known whereabouts, including the incidental fact that one of the terror-ists was a brother seeking vengeance. Michael dialed his satellite phone, telling the headquarters of the new developments. Within a few minutes, several elite Army Rangers formed a perimeter around the lookout station. An attack on civilians only esca-lated the charge these United States Army Rangers had to stop the terrorists.

The sky held several Apache helicopters. Each Apache's four titanium-fitted, twenty-foot blades beat the air searching for the enemy. These flying tanks were designed for war.

Within a few minutes, artillery fire echoed off of the moun-tain walls.

"Looks like they found their target," Michael said.

I was relieved. In the distance, the cat-and-mouse game ensued, as the terrorist's helicopter swept low into a ravine. The Apaches pursued their adversary with an unrelenting drive.

One of the pilots controlled the tail boom with his rear rotors, causing his Apache to hover, seamlessly flying in place, at the entrance of the ravine. Another helicopter circumvented the ridge, while the third sped to a distant edge of the ravine, block-ing the small black helicopter from escape.

In an unbeatable turn of events, the Apache on the ridge, lowered itself straight down, cracking tree limbs as it swept the narrow canyon's sides, maneuvering on top of the lone helicop-ter. Once it was pinned down, at a safe distance, the Apache launched skyward, firing it with two hell-fire missiles in succinct succession through its wake.

"It's over," I murmured.

The fireball, where the enemy's helicopter had once been, glowed reddish-orange, followed by a huge plain of smoke billowing skyward. The Apache helicopters swept the sky then turned to fly back to the base. Michael saluted them as the Apaches reached our lookout tower. The pilots toggled their blades, lowering sideways, sweeping to the left, as a man would have tipped his hat.

Katy, Lizzy, and Rock ran out to the railing, shouting and waving their appreciation.

The Army Rangers posted as centuries on the ground acknowledged the Apaches with raised fists of triumph.

Rock, Katy, and Lizzy shouted from the lookout railing, "We won!"

"They shot them down!"

"It's over!"

The inside of the cab where Michael and I stood was quiet. Michael held me for a moment, both of us silent. I felt detached from everything around me.

"Is it really over?" I asked, searching Michael's eyes.

Michael's determined chin jutted down, his arms flexed as they wrapped me tighter. "It's over."

"How do you think they got to us?"

"Those guys were probably on the watch list. They must have traveled under fake passports or were smuggled in."

"You think that this will change the way I live? Do I need to go into hiding? Like witness protection or something?"

"Miranda, you can't live like that forever. Security will be tighter for every airport, train station, and border crossing. You and your family will be assigned extra security for a while. Things will calm down. No matter what, I will never stop protecting you and watching for anything that could harm you or the children. God is with us too. You know firsthand of His sovereign protection. You asked me if this is over. It may never be fully over. The War on Terrorism began because of an act of hatred against

America. Hate will always be with us because people have forsaken God. I'm sorry, I wish I could be more certain of the future."

"We do have something else to fight hate with," I said.

"What's that?" Michael asked seriously.

"We have love," I said, looking into his green eyes.

"Our love for each other is the strongest tie I've seen," Michael said, touching my face.

"I agree, and I believe with all my heart that the tie is only growing stronger," I said emphatically.

Michael kissed me softly. I leaned against him for a moment, letting his strength seep into my weariness.

"You guys ready to get out of here?" Rock said as he beckoned with his arm. "The Army Rangers on the ground have promised an escort to get us off the mountain range and safely to base."

"Can you come too, Michael?" I asked, expecting him to say he would be along later.

"Yes, I can. I'm not letting my beautiful girl go back without me!"

I smiled at him as he gathered his belongings, emptying some trash into his duffel bag, leaving the place spotless.

"How's your arm and leg? Do you think you can manage?"

"It's sore, but I think I'm up to it."

Rock, Lizzy, and Katy were almost halfway down. I stepped out on the crisscross-patterned steel platform, feeling some pain stiffen my left leg as I began making my way down the stairs.

"It's doable," I said to Michael, smiling and trying to be positive.

I made my way to the bottom, and as my feet touched the ground, I took a moment to breathe. Today had been a very long day. To get home, we would need to hike out about five miles. I felt tired at the thought. We hiked one mile to the east, then headed south, the wind swept nightfall on us and settled the dusky pale sky outlined only by a flimsy moon crescent.

I had to admit, the Army Rangers were in rare form. Their humor and good attitude bolstered my exhausted limbs. Lizzy seemed in her element, surrounded by the striking young men. Having grown up with lots of brothers, she had a tomboy attitude combined with a natural sense of humor. She was also quite pretty in an unpretentious way. One of them paid particular interest to her. *Mmm, that may be interesting for her.*

We descended quicker than I expected, driven by the adrenaline of the victorious outcome of the day. Arriving near the base lodge, a medic saw to our wounds. We each needed a few stitches, plus a round of antibiotics, topical cream, a tetanus shot and some wound care. Katy and I were sore, but would recover with very little scarring. Katy was quite a trooper. Despite her "blonde" moments that I'd witnessed at the coffee shop, she held it together and came across as very brave and mature. She was growing up, and I was proud of her and thankful for her friendship.

Michael drove us about ten miles to the parking lot where our cars were located. I insisted on driving my Jeep home, knowing that I needed to be alone. I wanted to spend time with my King. In some ways, I felt angry about what happened today. Why does this keep happening? Is there a way out?

God, can I say that I'm a little mad at you or at least at the situation you've allowed? I feel like those terrorists should have been out of my life. Let me say, I'm shaken to my core that my plans have been put aside to deal with the enemy, over and over again. What is your purpose? Sometimes, as a single mom, I feel like I am barely holding on, between work, the kids, their needs, and now another enemy attack...I'm spent. I'm exhausted. I'm done.

I cranked up the Christian music by Evervine, letting the words wash over me:

> Set your face toward heaven.
> Leave your worries at the Cross.
> Trust in God forever, He is with you.
> Oh, I love you Father, forevermore.

As the lyrics of the music ministered to me, my heart turned toward God.

Wow, God. I think you answered this angry girl just now. I believe that you are speaking to me to put down my anger and give my needs to You, lay them at the cross, and see how You are already working and answering prayers.

I worshiped God and celebrated the victories that He had accomplished in my own life. After a while, I turned the music off and glanced at the night sky. The stars twinkled in unending numbers, proclaiming the work of God's hands. The quiet peace of God flowed over me, bringing comfort after such a brutal day.

God, thank you for my miracle You provided for me today. I know that even in the smallest part of my life, You are there. You showed Your power to me in a palatable way today that is beyond my comprehension. I am eternally grateful to You. My life is in Your hands. I praise You God, my King!

It is written in Mark 8:36, "What good is it for someone to gain the whole world, yet forfeit their soul?" If all I seek is security and to have all my needs met, I missed the point in what God is doing. He is using the difficult times, the unbelievable attacks from the enemy, and the desperate cries for help from my heart to draw me nearer to Him. He is providing in my weakness. The Lord is peace, Jehovah-Shalom.

We were safe, at last. My town, my children, and I could walk the streets again, knowing that we would be alive and protected. I knew God was with me, blessing me. He had watched over me. He had sent Michael to protect me and the fine people of Mountain View.

The children were spending the night at my parents' house, and I had already communicated to them briefly about my ordeal. I was so glad to arrive home and climb into bed that night, weary, worn, but thankful. My body needed rest; my heart, however, recognized God's mercies and justness. He was my shelter in the storm of life. He overshadowed me and reigned over me. I was a daughter of this sacred King and I was thankful for His provisions for my life. I no longer sought a perfect day, just one that gave me the opportunity to thank Him for His goodness and cry out to Him for His saving power.

Though the enemy had drawn up against me numerous times God had been with me. Even the day-to-day pressures of being a single mom would all be met by my provisional Lord. "He sought me and bought me with His redeeming love," as the old familiar hymn "Victory in Jesus" says. I was His, by the blood stained verdict of forgiveness from Jesus on the cross. With all my being and love for Him, I will stand and be firm in what I know is truth. I will overcome, through His power, and will see another day through.

Lord, I pray, one more minute of my life, is spent with you. One more second, I get to be with you. I will be refreshed and made alive, renewed over time and one day, one beautiful day all things will pass away as heaven shines brighter. My eternal home is secure, for my resting place is in You. Nothing I do will separate myself from you, O my God...I love you. Amen. Good night, God.

Chapter 22

I had taken a few days off from work due to the fact that I was giving statements to agents of the Terrorism Task Force Division and needed to recover from my injuries. By midweek, I had regained mobility and felt less stiff so I could return to Bean Me Up. The instant I walked in, the warm smell of coffee greeted my nose. The cheerful drip of the coffee percolating from one of our four industrial-size coffee makers inspired me to whip up a caramel latte for myself. I was actually glad to be back at work and try something straightforward for a change. In spite of the busyness at the shop, Carrie and I had a few minutes to catch up in between customers.

"Miranda, what a weekend! You've been through too much. I've been praying for you."

"Thanks. You know I am truly amazed at how God has provided for me this past weekend. He was with me every step of the way."

"Psalm 23:4 states, 'Even though I walk through the darkest valley, I will fear no evil, for you are with me; your rod and your staff, they comfort me,'" Carrie said.

"That verse of scripture was in evidence this weekend. I was in a dark place, but He was still with me. God Almighty is with us all. We only have to trust Him, knowing that His presence is already in the midst of us."

"What is this world coming to with all the terrorist attacks near our town of Mountain View?" Carrie posed the question that I had been pondering.

"I know. It's not like we have any famous government buildings or important historical locations. We just have people. People who love America and who are now starting to renew their love for God."

"If nothing else, having the enemy in our town has put our community on high alert for dangerous activity. People have felt that they are no longer in control of their safety, like they once were. Dependency upon God had increased. Just this past Sunday, the church had to put in more chairs at the back of the sanctuary."

"I noticed that, too. What a good 'problem' to have!" I nodded in cheerful agreement.

Chapter 23

Though I had met Michael's parents, Frank and Hil, a few times this past year, I had never been to their house. Michael and I drove up to meet them for lunch one Saturday. It was a joy to see the home that Michael grew up in. Their town of Juniper was a suburb of Salix. At one time, their outlying ranch-style house was located in empty grasslands, marked only by stately plateaus and distant white-capped mountains. However, times had changed, and the area had grown up around them. Businesses had come to the once rural town, streets were developed, churches and schools had been added.

Michael's mom, Hil (short for Hilda), gave me a tour of her home. I imagined Michael's feet as they had pitter-pattered along the elongated halls that linked the bedrooms, down to the living room and then up to the kitchen.

"We've been here for forty years," Hil said as we walked through the living room.

The classic wood paneling had been updated with paint the color of a warm eggshell. The trim and ceiling were painted the same, creating a monochromatic hue that was both light and spacious.

"It's lovely. I could spend many a day here."

The wide windows at the back of the house captured the faraway mountain range like a giant viewfinder, each window selecting a separate shot of the world. I breathed in and smiled at Hil. Their little world was a home in every sense of the word. I imagined one day that Ruston and Becca might visit here and could create new memories for Hil and Frank, setting perhaps a new realm to their defined space but, I knew, always welcomed.

We ate steak in the backyard, which Michael and Frank had grilled along with some marvelous sides that Hil had created with magazine-worthy results. His mom was also quite the gardener. Heather, blue flax, wild lupine, hostas, alongside river rocks of varying size, surrounded us. Though planted, the backyard held a wild, natural beauty as native plants, clustered with herbs, blossoming annuals, and heavenly scented petals weaved a lovely scene.

"I can't believe I'm in a backyard. I should be paying you for a stroll through your gardens," I said, taking in the lovely surroundings.

"It is a wonderful way to enjoy the beauty of God's world," Hil said, happy that I enjoyed her labor of love.

Frank offered me some lemon water as I leaned back in my ivory painted wrought iron chair.

"Thank you. So, Frank, what do you do these days?"

"Besides listen to this gal over hear and keep up with her honey-dos…I play golf with some old guys from church."

Hil tittered about her honey-do list and teasingly wrote a few things on her napkin then threw it into Frank's lap. We laughed at their antics. They obviously had a strong bond, filled with humor and devotion.

"Michael, do you play golf as well?" I asked.

"Not really, I haven't had the time. But Dad is pretty good."

"Shot a level-par seventy-five last week. That's good for me," Frank said.

"I don't know much about golf, but that's really good, isn't it?" I asked, impressed.

"Well, the pros are at fifty and most people are around one-hundred. For an eighteen-hole golf course, I'd say a seventy-five was a miracle, for me!" Frank said with a laugh.

"Frank, you are funny!" I said as I brought a forkful of Hilda's fudge dessert to my mouth. "Hil, this dessert is wonderful," I said.

"Chocolate fudge is my specialty. Sometimes in the winter, I play around with different ingredients, but I wasn't sure if you liked nuts or not, so I kept it plain."

"Of course she likes nuts. She likes Michael!" Frank laughed, slapping his knee.

I chuckled under my breath while Hil crinkled her nose at Frank.

"Well, I don't know if I'm crazy unless you count how I feel about Miranda!" Michael pulled me to his side as I bit my lower lip and blushed.

"You two are so cute together. Frank, remember when we were young and in love?"

"Hil, we still are!" Frank said, encircling Hil's trim waist and kissing her cheek.

We stayed until the crickets had begun their song. The twilight sky was lavender gray and held whispers of clouds in its cloak. The moon would rise soon, and the velvet black robe would sweep the color from the sky.

I leaned my head back on my headrest while Michael drove and thought about the future.

"You did great, you know. My parents adore you!"

"I love them too. Especially since they did such an amazing job raising you."

"We're blessed, you and I, because we both have wonderful parents. The bar has been raised high," Michael said.

"They are a good example and encouragement for the values of lasting love," I replied, nodding demurely.

Inside I was praying that God would show us when our enduring love song would truly begin. I was ready to get this gig on the road. It was late August and Michael's patience had surprised me in our journey. I hoped that soon he would be inspired by God to ask me to marry him. Surely, he knew by now how I felt about him. I didn't want to be impatient, but this past year felt like infinity.

"Lord, please give me patience as I wait on your timing."

Two weeks after our dinner with Michael's parents, Michael took me on a beautiful hike, with trees that had begun to change their leaves to gold, crimson, and orange. He had packed creamy potato soup in a thermos and acquired a box of divine desserts from a local bakery.

"How about we rest here by this waterfall and enjoy our picnic?"

Spreading a cozy, plaid, fleece blanket out, we sat down. I was feeling so peaceful and full of joy by the rushing stream. I looked at Michael as he gazed into my eyes, completely smitten. His eyes and smile were bright with love. In a moment, he reached into his backpack and unzipped an inner compartment. His hands held an opened white velvet box that had a princess-cut, two-carat diamond with a halo surround, platinum setting.

"Is this real? I mean…of course it's real, I…wait…did you ask me something?" I said, breathing rapidly with my hands reaching for the ring.

"I'm getting to that," Michael said with a laugh. "Miranda, will you marry me and carry my heart with you forever?"

"Yes!" I said as I leaped into Michael's arms and kissed him.

"Miranda, I love you," Michael said.

"I love you too. You're sure about this? You want me, my kids, my aptness in finding trouble, and my inability to cook?" I asked as I searched his face.

"Yes, I want it all. Burnt toast is my favorite! Miranda, I have been amazed every day by you since we met. I don't think cooking is going to be a deal breaker. I love you in every way possible and want you to be my wife forever." Michael held my face gently and kissed me again.

My broken heart, after all those years of hurt, washed away. I was loved by my Heavenly Father and this wonderful, amazing man of God.

"You know," I said, hugging Michael, "this means that we have forever love. We've already been through the—*or worse* part, so maybe the—*for better* is all yet to come!"

Afterward, on the drive to my parents' house Michael shared with me the steps that had led him to receiving my dad's blessing on our engagement.

Michael had talked to my dad the week after we had dinner with his parents and told him jokingly, "I'm not letting this girl get away. In all seriousness, sir, I love her and believe that God has brought us together for good, to accomplish His purposes." Michael then recited Jeremiah 29:11, "'For I know the plans I have for you,' declares the LORD, 'plans to prosper you and not to harm you, plans to give you hope and a future.' Miranda is a part of my hope and future. I know that I am *always* going to love and protect her and the children. I love your family and Miranda and we belong together forever. Sir, I'm asking for your daughter's hand in marriage."

Dad, of course, said, "Yes, I give you my blessing. We are glad to call you, *son*."

My prayer for patience was to be rewarded. I guess God had been waiting for that prayer.

Afterward, we went by Mom and Dad's house to have supper and pick up Ruston and Becca.

"Giselle and I have been busy in the kitchen," Mom said, her face warm from the stove.

"I'm learning to make your mom's gumbo and potato salad," Giselle said while stirring the soup in a circular motion with a long wooden spoon.

"The secret to my gumbo is the stirring! When you make a roux, the flour has to be stirred constantly until it is dark brown. Otherwise, your gumbo will not have an authentic brown broth," Mom said.

"I think my arm is about to fall off," Giselle complained with mirth.

"Well, then you know it's about done. Will you stir for a moment, honey? I'm about to drain the potatoes," Mom asked me, pointing to the large, stainless steel gumbo pot.

"Sure, this brings back memories. When I was little, I loved the smell of your chicken and sausage gumbo. Gumbo can be eaten any time of year, even in the summer. I love it so much. In the South, we would add fresh Gulf shrimp too, but that's a little hard to come by here. Oh, and just wait until you taste Mom's potato salad. We would plop it right in the middle of our gumbo!" I said, giving the gumbo a stir.

"In the gumbo?" Giselle inquired.

"It adds a wonderful flavor and texture," I said.

"Now, Giselle, when you add the mayonnaise to the potato salad, you must add it in while the potatoes are warm. This will make it super creamy. After stirring, put in green onions for a bit of lagniappe," Mom instructed.

"Lan-yap?" Giselle looked confused.

"A little something extra. That's how we say that with one Cajun-French word," Mom said. "Hey, dawlin', can you come here a minute, it's about ready!" Mom called to Dad from the other room.

Dad walked in and grabbed some bowls out of the cupboard. "Is it time?"

Giselle and I looked at each other and I whispered, "Just watch."

Dad scooped Mom up in his arms and kissed her. "There's the love for the pot," Dad said, holding her for another moment.

"So that's why everything tastes so good around here," Giselle whispered to me with a smile.

Dad sprinkled the seasoning file´ on the top of each bowl after Mom dished the gumbo into them. We ate in the long dining room, bowls clanked as the spoons hit the bottoms. Conversation flowed easily, sprinkled with laughter. Michael and I looked at each other and then shared our good news.

"We're engaged!" we said together.

"What?"

Everyone got up from the table to hug us. The ladies grabbed my hand to gawk at the ring (that I had slipped back on my finger).

"We are so happy for you!" Mom and Dad said, hugging me.

"I'm excited for you too!" Becca said while doing her usual ecstatic jumps and claps.

"Whoo-hoo! This is great, now it's official. Michael can hang out with us all the time!" Ruston said, hugging Michael and then me.

"I love you too."

Michael squeezed Becca, Ruston, and I in a group hug.

We couldn't be happier or more thankful to God that had brought about His miracle called—family.

Chapter 24

On the one year anniversary to when I had first met Michael, I got dressed for a very special date. The kind of date that hopefully wouldn't involve climbing gear, guns, or bullets. If everything went according to plan, today would just be a day of flowers, photographs, dancing, and "I do's."

I looked at my dress cascading in the mirror. I had chosen a designer gown that had a V-neck, sleeveless bodice, with ombre tulle the color of spilled cream, swept to one side and fastened with an antique brooch.

Turning, I stood looking at the mountains out my windows, remembering the time that Michael came and played with the children in the snow. That had been the season of my life when I began to imagine being loved by Michael. I touched my curls partially drawn up and clasped with ivory sweetheart roses. He chose me. Wow! I couldn't believe it.

"Miranda, do you have a minute?" Mom came into the room with her arms full.

"Oh my, flowers?" I said.

"Look at this beautiful arrangement from you-know-who," Mom said with her eyes misting as she took in my dress.

My eyes surveyed pink peonies, purple heather, orange Gerbera daisies, yellow snapdragons, soft peach tulips, and one white rose. Attached was a note written in a masculine, thin, sloping handwriting.

"Miranda. Dear one, I am so in love with you, I can hardly believe that we are here on this long-awaited day. I am so thankful that you love me. You see me and you know me. You are my heart and you have given me hope for happiness. I love you, forever. Always yours, Michael. PS: I can't wait to see you in a little while. I'll be the guy in the tux at the front."

I held the note close to my heart. "He is sweet, isn't he?"

Mom came over and touched my shoulder. "He is a dawlin', he really is. Now, let's get your dad up here." Mom called from the top steps, "Honey, you are going to want to see this."

Dad walked up the creaky, wooden stairs slowly. "I'm not sure I'm ready... Oh, sugar, you look beautiful." Dad hugged me in a gentle fashion. "I was saying that I'm not sure I'm ready for this. You're our little girl. This is a big day for all of us. Are you sure you like this guy?" my dad said, half teasing.

"Dad, you know me and you know Michael now. Is there any doubt in your mind? I am completely confident that God brought us together. Our Heavenly Father has been our whole center and foundation for this relationship," I said.

"I know, baby, a dad just has to ask. I love you and I love Michael. Your mom and I support this marriage 100 percent," he said as he kissed the top of my head.

I hugged Dad and said, "Good, I want your support all the way."

"Well, you've got it, Miranda. There is no doubt. We are with you!" Dad said with meaning.

When they flung open the doors, and the music rose in the church, I saw Michael beaming a brilliant smile at me. The flowers were arrayed in elaborate spreads and the pewter candelabras flickered with their waxing captors. Carrie, Lizzy, Katy, and Giselle were dressed in seafoam colored shift dresses. Ruston and Becca were on the lower stairs around the altar. I breathed in as we glided past friends and family. I felt like I was on a cloud as my dad kissed my cheek and joined my hands with Michael. Dad then gave the pastor his and Mom's blessing. Michael and

I looked at each other, joy beyond belief spreading in our hearts and onto our faces.

"For better or for worse…as long as we both shall live," we both recited in love.

Our reception was held in the large outdoor courtyard of the beautiful restaurant that we ate at for our "official" first date. The stone walls and arches framed the mountain backdrop splendidly. The sky was vividly painted blue with the sun spread brightly in a glittering array. Its golden hues warmed the stones and river rocks bordering the flower beds. Garden flowers spilled out of wire baskets along with long ivy vines trailing the ground. Our three-tiered cake adorned in pink peonies and delicate almond butter cream loops looked delectable. The kids were so excited. Becca twirled to the music, the garland in her hair had flowers and ribbons intertwined. Her sash and skirt sprayed out in abandon, like the campanulate form of a bell. Ruston was eyeing the cake, so before he could swipe some icing, I asked him to dance with me.

"I would be honored, my lady," Ruston answered me in a contrived English accent.

"How fine of you," I said in the same silly manner. We danced for a moment and Ruston whispered.

"I am happy for you and Michael. This is good for all of us."

"Thank you, Ruston. I believe it is as well. I love you very much," I said.

"I love you too, Mom," Ruston said as he hugged me.

"Mrs. Michael Taylor, I presume." Michael had seized the moment to cut in, which was okay with Ruston. He was happy to go wander toward some of his friends at the buffet.

"Major Michael Taylor. I have found you a bride and it is me!" I said, blinking my lashes.

Michael whispered a few things to me that were just between us and then we kissed a tender kiss that I was only too happy to receive.

"We better cut that cake and get out of here," Michael said. "I believe there is a honeymoon after a wedding."

"Yes, there is, and since the groom has been so obliged to keep secrets, I think it would be good to get this show on the road," I said without hesitation. The light, fluffy cake with the melt-in-your-mouth sugary icing hit my lips. "Mmm. This makes it all worth it," I said, savoring my cake sample Michael had fed me.

"Hey, what about me?" Michael pouted. I brought the cake to his lips, and his lips brushed my fingers. "Okay, this *is* worth it!" Michael announced. Everyone cheered as people lined up for cake. I'll be honest, men and kids endured weddings for the cake. This slice of heaven covered in almond buttercream icing pleased everybody's palate, including Mrs. Liddenaul's.

"This cake is quite good, Miranda…and you look very pretty," Mrs. Liddenaul said.

"I'm so glad you could come and celebrate with us," I replied warmly, as only a bride can do on her wedding day.

"It was very thoughtful of you to invite some of the gentlemen and I from the coffee shop. It meant the world to us, absolutely the world!"

I saw Mr. Oaklan beckon to Mrs. Liddenaul and she seemed to blush slightly.

"I'm sorry, but if you'll excuse me, Mr. Oaklan has promised me a dance."

I stood with my mouth slightly agape and thought, *God, I shouldn't be surprised at how beautiful Your love and kindness can grow.*

After we visited with all the family and friends, Michael told me that we needed to get going. I said good-bye to Mom, Dad, Hil, Frank, Ruston, and Becca.

"We will be okay. Gramma and Papa have lots of fun things planned for us too!" Becca said, buoyed with confidence as Gramma put her arms around her.

"Bring us a souvenir!" Ruston said with a laugh.

"I love you too, Ruston. Help Gramma, okay?"

"I will and I'll keep an eye on Becca."

"You hear that, Becca? Eyes on Ruston, he might need some supervision," Michael said in jest.

Both kids grinned as we hugged them one more time. Telling them I loved them again, I turned to see much of the family and friends had filtered under the archways and began to throw flower petals at us. Michael gathered me up in his arms and carried me down the stone pathway. My dress trailed over to one side and onto the path, lingering lightly among the flower petals. Arriving at his granite-colored SUV, he opened the door, and I got in the passenger side. Michael tucked my dress into his vehicle, shut the door, then ran to his driver's side, and we sped off. I waved to everyone and blew kisses from my open window.

As we rounded the corner, and headed toward the interstate, Michael turned to me and said, "Do you want this honeymoon mystery solved?"

"More than ever," I replied, smiling.

"Tonight we are staying in Salix in an amazing hotel with tons of luxurious amenities. A pool, hot tub, and a beautiful suite with a western vantage point of the mountains. Our ultimate destination is St. Lucia. Tomorrow we fly to the Caribbean island in the tropics known for a volcano, lush tropics, sandy, white beaches, and hiking trails!" Michael said happily as he unfolded a brochure for me to review.

"We'll see about the hiking, does it involve climbing gear?" I teased.

"No, but you can hike to some gorgeous waterfalls or we can relax at the beach. Plus, we have a bungalow that overlooks the water. I think we will find plenty to occupy us," Michael said with his eyes twinkling.

The steady rhythm of the drive down the interstate lulled me after such a wonderful but hectic day, as I thought about how marriage was and always will be a magnificent endeavor. When God is first in the relationship, pure love will always grow stronger. Aiding our marriage to last through the tips and turns of life, the Word of God would be our foundation. I knew that our marriage wouldn't be perfect, but I knew that God was with us and had drawn us together. I had hope that we could always see past each other's faults to the heart of who we loved and had first met. Hopefully, as we both matured, we would become more Christlike and our love for each other would blossom, akin to a morning glory opening its petals with the dayspring's mist.

I opened my hands and stretched them toward the sun. My ring sparkled and I was in awe. *I was married.* I believe with God that Michael and I could experience love in all its fullness. The agape love that God Himself showed us. I thought of the verses from 1 Corinthians 13 recited at our wedding, "Love is patient, love is kind…It always protects, always trusts, always hopes, always perseveres. Love never fails." Truth be told, I was glad to go on our long-awaited honeymoon with my best friend—Michael! I think he sensed my thoughts as he reached over and held my hand.

The late afternoon's sun crept in through the tinted windows of the SUV. I noticed the celestial cerulean that covered the sky, likened to a giant shower cap, which dismissed any clouds with a clever disguise.

I reached down and pulled out my purse-sized Bible. Flipping open to Isaiah 46:10–11, I began reading aloud, "I make known the end from the beginning, from ancient times, what is still to come. I say, "My purpose will stand, and I will do all that I please." From the east I summon a bird of prey; from a far-off land, a man to fulfill my purpose. What I have said, that I will bring about;

what I have planned, that I will do.' Michael, I've dreamed for so long of a beautiful future. It is such a comfort that God's purposes stand and he does what pleases Him. I thank God that He thought of you to fulfill His purposes. I am astounded and amazed at the way God brought me so much good. Now that you married me, I wonder what other good things are to come?"

I noticed Michael's left hand on the steering wheel tighten. My eyes swept over to his ring on his left ring finger, which looked polished in its platinum setting. The ring was permanent, like our love for each other.

He glanced at me with a smile that went to his eyes. "God has prepared amazing adventures for us as we explore life—together. Miranda, I don't know everything in the future, but I do know that I love you. I thank God that He fulfilled all my dreams with you, too! You are one astounding woman! As far as the verses you shared a minute ago...Amen! We both have a unique plan that God intended for us from the beginning of time. God has extended His purposes, one-hundred–fold, when He created you and our marriage! Everything we have been through has been filtered by a loving Father who has determined our future, together. His purpose will stand the test of time, that's why our marriage will be forever on this earth. God is pleased to accomplish His work and establish the work of His hands. We will always remain in His love."

"God really shined His love today at our wedding," I said, remembering the resplendent blossoms and mountain-crested skyline.

"The wedding day is just a taste of what heaven will be like, when the sky opens up and we are caught up with Him in glory. Colossians 3:4 tells us, 'When Christ, who is your life, appears, then you also will appear with him in glory,'" Michael said.

The sun began to set, warming me with its fiery rays.

"Oh wow!" I breathed.

We blinked as the red and orange sphere outlined the mountains then slipped down to sleep. "Look, we really are driving off into the sunset," I said quietly as I leaned over to kiss my husband.

It was now just our beginning, but it had started a long time ago.

Discussion Guide

The questions below can be discussed as a group or provide you with a personal study for your enrichment.

1. What did Miranda believe about herself after the divorce?

2. How did she learn to trust God and find her purpose?

3. How did Miranda's family and Michael help her in building her confidence?

4. In what ways did Miranda grow in her belief that God was in control of her life?

5. Why does God use difficult circumstances in our lives to cry out to Him? What are some personal struggles and trials God used for good in your own life?

6. If you have gone through a divorce or have a close friend or family member that has, what life lessons have you learned?

7. List some spiritual truths that are found in Psalm 16:5-7, "Lord, you have assigned me my portion and my cup; you have made my lot secure. The boundary lines have fallen for me in pleasant places; surely I have a delightful inheritance. I will praise the Lord, who counsels me; even at night my heart instructs me."

8. Discuss some ways God answered prayers through difficult times in your life?

9. What does God promise in Psalm 34:18? "The Lord is close to the brokenhearted and saves those who are crushed in spirit" (Psalm 34:18).

10. Why does the Psalmist remind God of His unfailing love? "Help me, Lord my God; save me according to your unfailing love. Let them know that it is your hand, that you, Lord, have done it" (Psalm 109:26–27). Also, list some life experiences when you recognized God's hand in your life.

11. Explain why Proverbs 16:9 teaches us about the Sovereignty of God?

"In their hearts humans plan their course,
but the LORD establishes their steps"

12. Miranda questioned God's plans for her life. What exchange did God have with Gideon in Judges 6:11-16? Here is an excerpt: "Pardon me, my lord," Gideon replied, "...if the LORD is with us, why has all this happened to us?...The LORD answered, "I will be with you..." Recount an event in your life when this verse related to you?

13. Share how God has abundantly met your needs and showered His love on you. Read John 10:10 and Jeremiah 29:11 to better understand what type of life God desires for you.
    "The thief comes only to steal and kill and destroy; I have come that they may have life, and have it to the full" (John 10:10).
    "For I know the plans I have for you," declares the Lord, "plans to prosper you and not to harm you, plans to give you hope and a future" (Jeremiah 29:11)

Can you believe it? God loves you so much. He is the peace you have sought every day of your stormy life. You might wonder, can God love me? I'm not perfect. I've made mistakes. Guess what? He loves you, just as you are. When you accept His Son Jesus into your heart, God forgives you and will enable you to walk with Him.

If you have never accepted Jesus as your Lord and Savior, would you like to? The Bible tells us, "For the wages of sin is death, but the gift of God is eternal life in Christ Jesus our Lord" (Romans 6:23).

"For God so loved the world that he gave his one and only Son, that whoever believes in him shall not perish but have eternal life. For God did not send his Son into the world to condemn the world, but to save the world through him" (John 3:16–17).

Pray with me now:

> Sweet Heavenly Father, I pray to receive Christ as my Lord (the one in charge of my life) and Savior right now. Thank you for forgiving my sins: past, present, and future. Thank you so much for dying on the cross and rising again. I give you my whole heart and life. In Jesus' saving name, amen!

If you prayed that prayer for the first time, write me and let me know. I also encourage you to get involved in a Bible-believing church where you can be encouraged. I love you, like a sister in Christ! Thank you for reading *Bean Me Up*. Now, go drink some coffee or tea, get in God's word, and encourage someone today!

Walk with the love of God,
Lauren Busbee
www.bowtieendings.com